A Wish Come True

Sunrise Sisters Trilogy

OLIVIA MILES

Rosewood Press

Also by Olivia Miles

Copyright © 2023 by Megan Leavell
ISBN 979-8-9862624-6-8

A Wish Come True

chapter one

Afternoons at the Sunrise Sisters Bakery were Jill Parker's favorite time of day—even more than the quiet mornings, when only she and her sisters occupied the kitchen, preparing their baked goods, experimenting with new recipes for specials, and pulling tray after tray out of the ovens, each treat smelling better than the last.

By the time the after-school rush ended, the pastry case was very picked over, the tables were freeing up, and there was a feeling of a job well done. And a day well spent. Little other than a perfectly flakey croissant and a creamy coffee was as satisfying in her mind.

Today, Jill sank onto a stool in the kitchen to rest her legs, caffeinate, and taste one of her favorite bakes—a slice of cinnamon streusel cake—while her sisters worked the front counter.

Her youngest sister, Carly, might enjoy coming up with colorfully decorated cookies or confetti-style cakes that appealed to the younger crowd, but Jill still treasured her grandmother's recipes the most. A slice of streusel cake, much like their strawberry pie, was hardly something that brought in the new business lately, but to Jill, it was perfect.

And comforting. And a reminder that while a lot had changed in Hope Hollow and in the bakery in recent months, some things would always stay the same.

"We just sold the last brownie!" Carly announced, pushing through the kitchen door.

"Does Becca need help out front?" Jill asked, knowing that Carly had arranged to leave early today to take her boyfriend's daughter, Daisy, to her weekly dance class.

Carly untied her apron strings with a shake of the head. "Only a few stragglers are left. But we'll probably have enough left over for a donation tonight."

Jill perked up at this. It was tradition for the bakery to box up whatever hadn't sold that day and give it to a local community center or cause. With the recent improvements they'd made to the bakery, they rarely had enough leftovers to give away, which was both a good and a bad thing, depending on how Jill thought about it.

"The animal shelter where Nana got her puppy might appreciate a treat," she said. Jill knew that her grandmother liked to say that she got the dog as a wedding gift for her new husband Robert, who lost his Labrador shortly before their early summer wedding, but it was clear that the little pup had won over both of his new owners. Nana even baked dog treats now—something she'd never even considered in the past.

"Speaking of Nana, have you given any more thought to her birthday this year?" Carly asked.

Jill sipped her coffee, wanting to enjoy it before it turned cold. "No, I've been too busy."

Carly, being Carly, gave her a pert look. According to Carly, who managed to work full-time at the bakery, date her old flame, spend time with little Daisy, and go out for wine with her best friend Joanna, all while still visiting their grandmother at least twice a week, Jill wasn't busy at all.

But then, Carly had always made time for a personal life, back when she was eighteen and dating Nick Sutton for the first time around, and then later when she left for college and took a job working for a magazine in Philadelphia for six years after that. Jill had been the one to come into the bakery every morning before dawn, work in the kitchen with their grandmother and sister Becca, and put in long days keeping the family business going—and that didn't leave much time for anything else.

Jill stifled a sigh, knowing that she and Carly had butted heads in the past over their duty to the bakery—and their vision for it. Her baby sister had proved her wrong last spring when she'd moved back to town and suggested that they change up the menu and spruce up the storefront, but Jill couldn't bring herself to say that Carly was right in this instance. She was busy. Too busy most days, not that she was complaining. She loved this bakery. Just like her mother and grandmother had before her.

"Someone has to finish up here and prep for tomorrow on the days you leave early," Jill reminded her sister.

"Fair point." Carly hung her apron on the hook beside the framed photo of the "Sunrise Sisters" with their mother and grandmother, a daily reminder of the three generations of women who had baked in this kitchen, passing down cherished recipes that they still made to this day. "I'm just saying that now that I'm back in town and it's not just you and Becca anymore, you can lighten your schedule just a little bit. Maybe make some time for—"

"Don't say it!" Jill shook her head. Ever since she moved back to town, Carly had been pushing her to date, and now that Becca was reunited with her ex-fiancé, both of her sisters seemed determined to see her settle down, too. Or at least "make time" for romance.

It wasn't that Jill was opposed to it. She'd even quietly wished to find that special someone, every year on her birthday, when she blew out the candles, grateful that superstition made it easy to keep a secret. But it was there all the same, like a whisper in her heart, a hope that one day, she too would know the kind of love that her sisters had found.

"Can't you accept that I'm happy with my life?" she asked Carly, who didn't look convinced, but luckily, had somewhere to be, meaning she wouldn't be sticking around long to argue her point or convince Jill that she should use a dating website.

"You know, Daisy's little friend Sophia has a father who has a single brother," Carly informed her. "Sophia told me all about her single uncle the other day."

"Does he live in Hope Hollow?" Jill asked, if only to prove she had an open mind. When Carly shook her head, she said, "Does he live in the state of Connecticut?"

Again, Carly shook her head. "But he sounds nice! And if he looks anything like Sophia's dad—"

4

"When it's meant to happen, it will happen," Jill said, knowing what Carly was about to say, even as she swung her handbag onto her shoulder.

Carly gave her a long look as she set a hand on the door-knob and then sighed deeply. "If you say so!"

Jill gave a little smile as Carly left through the back door. She did say so. Even if she didn't always believe so.

Standing up, she set her empty plate and mug in the sink and walked back into the storefront, where the tables had cleared and Becca was already boxing up today's leftovers. There weren't many, which was a good sign, and an indication that business was consistent.

"I think it's safe to say that all the changes we've made around here have paid off," Becca said, echoing Jill's thoughts.

Jill nodded, even though it hadn't been easy to part with old habits and ways.

"Something was missing for a while. Carly was it." Becca handed over the bakery box, which contained less than a dozen pastries and cookies, but a nice variety.

"Mom would be proud of us," Jill said, matching Becca's sad smile. They'd both known loss at an early age, but working in the bakery, together, made things a little easier. "Though I do miss having Nana here."

"Says the woman who insisted she retire early," Becca reminded her with a rueful look.

"Only because of her arthritis," Jill insisted, feeling defensive. "You know her health is important to me."

"I know," Becca said kindly. She waved to the last customer as he pushed through the door, and walked around the counter to turn the locks and flip the sign. "Do you want me to prep tonight?"

Jill shook her head. "I don't mind staying." She did it most days, and unlike Becca, she had nowhere else to be. Her cottage had been empty for weeks now, ever since Becca had decided to move in with Jonah. He may still be Becca's ex-fiancé, but it was clear she'd be wearing his grandmother's ring again very soon.

"You sure? I can cover tomorrow then," Becca promised. "Jonah's busy overseeing the new seating installation tonight so it would be nice to help him out."

"Has he decided when he's officially opening the restaurant?" Jill knew that Jonah had been tirelessly working on transforming his parents' former bistro into his own for the past two months—and that it had been a dream for many years before that.

"Hopefully before the end of the month!" Becca's eyes were bright. "Maybe we can have Nana's birthday party there."

A party. And the first one Jill wouldn't be attending with Becca as her sidekick. Both of her sisters would have dates. And Jill would be flying solo.

With that weary thought, Jill walked back into the kitchen, Becca following closely behind.

"I thought I'd run over tonight's leftovers to the animal shelter after I'm finished up here." It would prolong the day, but Jill had always liked to be busy.

"I'm sure they'd appreciate that," Becca said. "Nana said it was a wonderful place."

Jill couldn't help but smile when she thought of how

smitten Nana and Robert were with their new puppy, a sweet little dog with a fluffy white coat named Sugar who was unabashedly spoiled by them both. Contrary to Jill's concerns, Nana was loving her retirement.

"I still can't believe that Nana got her first dog at the ripe age of—"

"Nope!" Becca put a finger to her lips. "Remember what Nana said at dinner last Saturday? We can celebrate her birthday, but only if we don't reveal her age."

"A promise is a promise. And I love your idea of hosting it at Jonah's new restaurant."

"I can't wait to tell him the good news!" Becca wasted no time hanging up her apron beside Carly's and pushing out through the back door, leaving Jill alone in the kitchen.

She was never really alone, though, not in the bakery, which was filled with memories of her mother's laughter, or the smell of her grandmother's pies baking in the oven. She had a system, one that involved making her rounds of the storefront, making sure that everything was in place, and then prepping dough and batter that would make the next morning easier. It was a task she'd done with her grandmother, right up until the day she'd retired, and long before that, with her mother. Sometimes, they'd work in silence, but other times her mother would tell stories, ones that Jill still thought about now, as she went through her familiar routine, the very one that the women who raised her had entrusted her with.

It was a warm evening, and by the time Jill locked up, a breeze had set in. The late summer sun felt good against her skin when she stepped outside. Even though the kitchen at the bakery could get warm, the fresh air felt different, and she breathed it in as she walked to her car, already planning her evening.

Her cottage was close, walkable from Main Street, but she didn't mind the drive out to the edge of town. Maybe she'd order takeout from Concetti's, and pick it up on her way back.

Then eat, by herself, in front of the television. She could practically hear Carly's tsk of disapproval.

Or maybe she'd eat out on her small porch, enjoying what remained of the beautiful weather, before autumn snuck up, bringing cool wind and shorter days.

Or maybe she'd just do what she always did lately, which was toss a salad, eat while chatting to her grandmother on the phone or watching a cooking show, and then retire to bed early with a good book.

The early mornings were always her excuse but now, as she drove away from the bakery, she considered her sisters' full lives. And she knew she was running out of excuses not to have that too—but it wasn't quite as simple as what Carly implied, was it?

What she wanted was the kind of love that would last forever.

And she knew all too well that this was something she would never find. That maybe, it didn't exist at all.

*

Frankie Concetti could hear the sobbing from the sidewalk patio where diners were trying tonight's special in peace. A few of the locals that he knew glanced up in confusion as he refilled their wine.

"You know Mamma," he said, trying his best not to show any concern. "Sometimes she likes to listen to the opera while she cooks."

Setting the bottle down on the table, he hurried back inside, toward the kitchen. He stopped before pushing through the swinging door, his heart seized with fear as his mind went through all the possibilities. It could be anything, he knew, from one of Mamma's sisters being sick (or worse) to their mozzarella distributor deciding to go out of business.

"Break it to me, Ma," he said when he worked up the courage to enter the room, taking a slow breath.

Mamma Maria, as she was fondly known around Hope Hollow, looked up at him with tear-filled eyes, swollen from crying.

"That was my sister, Diana," she sputtered.

Oh no. So it wasn't a cheese problem then. That he could handle. But this? A real crisis? He didn't even expect that over at the fire station where he volunteered a few shifts each week. He told himself he was trained, prepared for the worst, but now he stood there, not knowing what to say, wishing he could do something to make his mother stop crying.

"It's not... Is it... Did someone..." Oh, man. Just thinking it made his stomach heave. "Die?"

The word was out, barely audible, whispered as the cold hard fear washed over his body.

"They may as well have! Someone may have stuck a spear straight through my heart!" Mamma wailed. "It's your cousin Gia! She's...she's..." She blew her nose loudly

9

into the handkerchief embroidered with her husband's initials that she'd carried with her since his death, two decades ago.

"Dead?" Frankie whispered. Gia had always been one of Mamma's favorite nieces. In a family as big as theirs, there were bound to be favorites. As an only child, he was both the favorite son and the only one in the hot seat at times.

"Worse!" Mamma cried, and then, her voice rising the way it only did when he once dropped an entire tray of tiramisu, she cried, "She's getting married!"

Frankie watched as his mother heaved a loud sob into her handkerchief, muffling the sounds of her misery.

"Well, Mamma, I hope you didn't have this reaction when Diana called," he said, giving her a little smile.

It was met with angry eyes. Enough to make him stand a little straighter. Clearly, now was not the time for jokes.

"Gia is seven years younger than you, Frankie! And you know what that means, don't you?"

Frankie did know what it meant. He was the last of his ten cousins to settle down. He'd be the last to produce grandchildren. And Mamma was running out of patience.

"Look at you!" Mamma said, tossing up her hands. "My handsome son! Those eyelashes could make any girl jealous! That smile brings back the same ladies club every Friday night. But you know the problem with that, Frankie?"

Frankie shook his head. He was still thinking about the eyelash comment, and wondering if that was a good thing or not.

"They are married women, Frankie! Worse, they are *old* married women." Mamma gave a long whimper into her hanky. "Where are the young single women?"

"But Ma, you never like any of the ones I meet!" Frankie pointed out.

"Don't go blaming this on me!" Mamma hissed.

Frankie pulled in a sigh. It was true that for every girl that didn't meet Mamma Maria's standards, he found ten more faults in her. It wasn't that any of the women he dated were bad, they just weren't…something. He couldn't even define it. He just knew that when the right girl came along, he'd know. And he wasn't in a rush to settle down.

It was his mother who felt the clock ticking.

"By the time you give me grandchildren, I'll be too feeble to put them on my knee," she was saying now.

Ah, yes, the old, frail knee threat. He'd long ago stopped feeling guilty about that one.

"Mamma, you're far from old," he assured her.

"The same can't be said for you!" She blew her nose loudly. "Look at my son. My beautiful son. You're not twenty-five anymore! You're not even thirty! You're…you're…"

Thirty-four. Which was about ten years too long for his mother to have waited.

"When is the wedding?" he asked his mother, trying to understand what he was dealing with here.

"In three weeks," Mamma replied to his relief. She'd be upset for a few weeks, and then the wedding would happen, she'd end up dancing, drinking, and denying that she ever even had this reaction when he reminded her.

Which he wouldn't. Because the last thing he wanted to do was draw further attention to his single status.

"Three weeks?" Frankie tried to change the topic. "That seems quick."

"Two weeks from Saturday, technically. They wanted a summer wedding and unlike some"—she stopped to give him a pointed look—"they didn't want to wait another year to be settled."

"Still, three weeks. Don't some people spend years planning weddings?"

Frankie realized that he wouldn't have that option when Mamma's eyes went wide. No, he'd already taken long enough.

"That doesn't give us much time," Mamma suddenly announced, her eyes darting to the window where she seemed to lose herself in thought.

Frankie watched the marinara sauce on the stove start bubbling over and crossed the kitchen to lower the heat.

"Doesn't give us much time for what?" He checked the pizza oven, deciding that the two pies had a few more minutes to go, then he picked up two order tabs, double-checking them against the salads that were lined on the counter.

"I'll have to call Diana back first thing tomorrow and ask about the guest list and the seating arrangements," Mamma was muttering as she returned the hanky to her pocket and washed her hands. The tears had thankfully dried up, and when she added the pasta to the sauce, she was almost smiling.

Frankie felt fresh unease turn in his gut. He knew his mother. Very well. And he had a bad feeling about this.

"Gia probably has at least a few single friends left," Mamma was saying, her voice lifting with hope.

"Oh no," Frankie groaned. "No, Ma. We've talked about this. No setups. No blind dates."

Until now his mother has reluctantly agreed, or at least been discreet in her efforts, inviting an old friend and her twenty-something daughter into the restaurant on a night Frankie was serving, or insisting he run deliveries to the single women in town. She always knew who was dating whom, who might be breaking up, and who might soon no longer be available. Her connection with Debbie at the flower shop across the street aided in these efforts.

But something in her eyes was defiant when she looked up at him.

"Between me and my three sisters, we'll come up with something. A wedding is a perfect place to meet a wife. Every single girl there will be hoping to catch the bouquet! Why can't they reel you in, too?"

"Ma," Frankie warned.

But his mother wasn't listening to him as she hurried around the kitchen, plating food.

"You'd better get these to table six before they get cold," was all she said. With a broad, satisfied smile, she plated two bowls of pasta and handed them to him.

And as Frankie left the kitchen, he had the growing sense that he was in even more trouble now than when he'd entered it.

*

13

Jill carried the box of pastries into the lobby of the Paws for Hope shelter and set it on the front desk. "Hello, I'm Jill Parker, from the Sunrise Sisters Bakery."

"I know your grandmother!" the woman behind the desk said, standing to greet her. "She used to make this amazing pie…"

"Which flavor?" Jill joked, because it was true that Nana was known for her pies.

"I'm afraid I haven't gotten into your bakery in a while. You're usually closed by the time I finish up here."

"Well, it's always been a tradition of ours to donate whatever we don't sell each day to a good cause." Jill slid the box forward and watched the woman's eyes light up. "I just wish I'd stopped by sooner."

Terri, according to her name badge, popped the bakery box lid and gasped. "It's a good thing I'm not alone here this evening or I'd eat everything in this box. Chad is actually in the back, feeding a new litter of puppies we just got in."

Chad, was it? Feeling out the situation, Jill said, "Is that your husband?"

Terri hooted. "Oh, no! No. Chad's—" She stopped and gave Jill a pointed look. "Well, why don't you see for yourself? I'm sure Chad will be thrilled to meet the lovely young woman who brought us this wonderful surprise! He does have a sweet tooth, you know."

Could it be this simple, after all? Was she about to walk through a door and meet someone who would change her life the way Nick and Jonah and Robert had changed Carly's, Becca's, and Nana's?

"Okay, then!" Jill said, feeling a little breathless at the possibility.

She smoothed a few strands of hair from her face and picked up the pastry box, following Terri through a door and down a hallway, already thinking of how her sisters would react when she told them about this turn of events. She was just dropping off leftover cookies and there he was. The man of her dreams. With a sweet tooth, nonetheless!

She smiled as she followed Terri, but all fantasies stopped when Terri opened a door and there, holding a small chestnut-colored dog, was a boy of about eleven.

"Chad, look what the nice lady from the bakery brought us!" Terri exclaimed.

Lady. She'd gone from being a lovely young woman about to meet a handsome, age-appropriate man to the nice lady who gave sweets to children.

Trying to mask her disappointment she opened the box so he could see, feeling a little guilty about her initial response when the boy's face lit up.

"Look at that cupcake!" he said, reaching for it. He paused to grin at the swirly vanilla frosting—and for the little puppy he was holding to take an opportunistic lick.

Terri clucked, but Jill laughed. "Aw, he likes sweets too, does he?"

"He's the runt of the litter," Terri said. "We've been trying to get him to eat, and this is the first interest he's shown."

Now Jill's heart did swell with hope—not for the possibility of meeting a tall, handsome stranger who might silence Carly's comments for good, but for the help she might have given this little dog. She took in his round brown eyes, his tiny little black nose, and the wagging tail visible behind Chad's arm.

"I guess he's been holding out for something he likes," Chad said, taking a bite of the cupcake, not caring that the puppy had already sampled it.

"Or someone he likes," Terri commented, giving Jill a nod. "That tail hasn't stopped moving since you walked into the room."

"He likes you," Chad agreed through a mouthful of cake.

"Oh." Jill's gaze rested on the tiny dog, feeling a strange pull when he tipped his head and opened his mouth, revealing the smallest pink tongue. "I think...I think he's smiling at me!"

"Do you want to hold him?" Chad asked.

Terri took the box from Jill's hands and Chad set the puppy into them. Jill couldn't believe how light he was compared to the bakery box. It was like holding a handful of fur. Oh, and it was soft fur. She petted his back and held him to her chest, where he nuzzled his little face against her neck.

"What's his name?" she asked.

Terri shrugged. "Doesn't have one yet. We just got this litter this morning. If you'd come in this time a day ago, you wouldn't have met him."

Wouldn't have met him? Jill stroked the little body against her chest, feeling the rise and fall of his breath under her palm. Of all the days to have done the leftovers run, when usually Carly or Becca took care of that so Jill could stick around, wipe down tables, and prep even more batter and dough for the next morning.

"By this time tomorrow, he'll probably have a home," Terri continued.

Meaning if she'd come in tomorrow instead, she wouldn't have met him either. She'd never have even known that he existed. And now that she did… Jill wasn't sure how she could go back to the way she felt just a few short minutes ago, to a world without him in it.

"I'll take him," she blurted. Then, seeing Terri's eyebrows shoot up, she added, "I mean, if I can."

Jill's heart was racing in anticipation and fear because this wasn't like her, not at all. She didn't go around making impulsive decisions. She thought things through, weighed the pros and cons, and she was careful with making changes. She didn't walk into a shelter, see a dog, and claim him.

Yet she just had.

She held the puppy a little tighter, her chest tightening when she considered that he might already be spoken for, just when she'd found him.

"I usually let people take a look around, get a feel for all the dogs before they do their choosing," Terri said. "But you don't need to worry about that. This little fellow did the choosing for us."

Jill felt her shoulders sink in relief as the puppy snuggled closer. "So he's mine?"

"He's all yours," Terri said with a smile.

All hers. Jill pulled the little dog away and looked him

in the eye, her heart pulling so tight that for a moment she thought it might burst.

Full, she realized, holding him close again. Her heart was full.

And she hadn't even known that a part of it was missing.

She just knew that maybe this year, her birthday wish had come true—in the most unexpected way.

chapter two

Jill checked her watch as she ran out of the house, fumbling for her keys. The puppy's barks could be heard from the laundry room where she'd left him, along with his new bed, a few carefully chosen toys, and a water bowl, all of which she'd purchased on her way home last night. The sound became muffled when she closed the door, but that did little to stop it from tearing at her heart all the same.

"I'll be back in a couple of hours to take you for a walk," she promised again, even though she was aware she was talking to a door now, that her dog couldn't hear her, and that even if he could, would he understand?

She thought he did. When she'd set him in the room and locked the baby gate she'd also purchased into the doorjamb, the look in his dark eyes was nearly enough to make her do something she hadn't done in over four years: call in sick. Because that's how she felt right now. Sick at the thought of having to go to work. And just as sick at the realization that she was late.

A glance at her phone revealed two texts, one from each sister, asking if she was okay (Becca), or murdered by a serial killer (Carly).

She hopped into her car and drove as fast as she could without speeding until she finally pulled to a stop at the back of the bakery, exactly three minutes later. She wasn't even completely out of the car when she saw Carly's nose pressed against the screen door to the kitchen.

"Sorry, sorry," she said as she pushed inside, swapping her handbag for her apron.

Becca looked up from the counter where she was scooping muffin batter into a tin. "We were starting to get worried. It's not like you to sleep in!"

More like not sleeping at all. Her puppy had slept the entire drive home from the shelter yesterday, through the pet supply store, where she spent a small fortune on everything he would need (and far too many things she simply wanted), and then dozed off early after exploring his new home—only to wake her up to squeaky cries at eleven. Then again at one o'clock. And then only to claw at the small crate she'd put on the bed beside her until she finally admitted defeat and let him curl up next to her. He'd fallen straight to sleep while she'd lain awake, afraid to so much as close her eyes for fear that he might wake up and walk off the bed and fall onto the hardwood floor.

"You look a little…frazzled." Carly watched her suspiciously as she returned to her mixing bowl. "Is everything okay?"

Everything was far from okay. It was wonderful. And scary at the same time.

"Last night ended up being a little…unexpected." Jill quickly surveyed the kitchen, assessing what had already been baked, what was baking, and what still needed to be made.

Pulling a large mixing bowl from a shelf, she decided to start on the morning quiche.

"Oh?" Carly raised an eyebrow. "Do tell."

Becca looked confused. "Did something happen after you dropped off the donation last night?"

Jill didn't know how she could share the news when she could barely believe it herself. She was so tired that she hadn't completely come out of her fog.

"Actually, something happened at the animal shelter when I was dropping off the leftovers," she started.

Now Carly's eyes went wide. "Don't tell me. You met someone!"

Jill nodded along as she began cracking eggs. "You could say that."

"Jill!" Becca cried, the smile evident in her tone. "You met someone? Last night? And you're just telling us *now*?" She stopped talking only to exchange a glance with Carly. "Wait. Unless…"

Now Jill looked up to give her sister a look of annoyance. "Please, you know I'm not that type of girl. Besides, it's not what you're thinking."

Becca looked disappointed. "So you didn't meet a handsome bachelor?"

Jill couldn't help but smile when she remembered

walking into that room and seeing her little puppy's face for the first time.

"I met the guy of my dreams all right," she said, watching as her sisters' faces both lit up in shock and surprise. "And he has four legs and a tail."

The room fell silent as her sisters blinked, both trying to process this.

"Wait," Carly said. "Did you…did you get a cat?"

"A dog," Jill replied, then watched as their shock grew, along with the size of their eyes.

"You got a *dog*?" Carly exclaimed.

"You?" said Becca, still not quite recovered from this news. "You got a dog."

Jill nodded. "I did." She blinked now, realizing that it was true. She'd not only done it but said it. She had gotten a dog. Without any planning. Without any thought. She had gone and completely changed not just her routine but her entire way of life, all in one night.

"I still can't believe it myself," she admitted as her fatigue turned into panic. Her stomach dropped and her heart began pounding in rhythm with her whisk as she beat the eggs, a little harder than usual. "I…don't know what I was thinking."

And what had she been thinking? She'd promised him that she'd be back to take him for a walk after the morning bakes were taken care of—and she would. But since when did she leave the bakery in the middle of the day unless it was to make a delivery? She didn't even go out for lunch, but always ate right here, in this kitchen.

"I guess I wasn't thinking," she continued because her

22

sisters were both too shell-shocked to speak at the moment. "I just...felt."

Now Becca's face lifted into a smile. "Oh, I think I might cry. I mean, that's how it works, you know? Your head can tell you whatever it wants, but the heart knows what it must have."

Jill nodded along, aware that she was whisking the eggs into a froth now but she couldn't quite stop.

"I've never felt that way before," she said. "About...anyone. Or anything. If I'd gone in one day earlier or later, I would never have even met him, and now...I can't imagine my life without him in it."

"Well, details please!" Carly insisted. "What's his name? What does he look like?"

"I'm still thinking about names," Jill said. She set down her whisk and walked over to her handbag to retrieve her phone. She was surprised to see that she'd already taken three hundred and twelve pictures of him.

She held up her favorite, taken in the backyard last night where she'd tried without success to potty train him, and her heart felt like it would burst at the sight of that sweet face.

"Look at that tiny nose!" Becca set a hand to her heart.

When her sisters cried out and gushed over how adorable he was, Jill couldn't help but feel something she usually only experienced when a little kid complimented her baked goods: proud.

"This means I'll have to leave for a quick walk after the morning rush," Jill hedged. "And probably for lunch, too. And then a midafternoon break. I hope that's okay."

"Okay?" Becca took one more look at the photos on Jill's phone and went back to her muffins. "Jill, we've been telling you for months that it's okay to cut back a bit here. Between the three of us, we'll always have things covered. And you've stayed late plenty of times when Carly or I had plans."

It was true, all true, but Jill had never been on the other side before. Her entire life up until now had been within these four walls, and all the people she'd loved had been too.

But now there was someone new in her life. Back at her house. Waiting for her to come home.

Giving her a reason to go back. And for the first time, this bakery, wonderful as it might be, wasn't everything to her anymore. And that was a very strange feeling indeed.

*

After Jill ran home to check on the puppy for the second time, walked him, cleaned up his mess, and gave him food and fresh water, she was starting to feel a little more in control, a place that she admittedly liked to be, even if her sisters often teased her about it.

"How did Jonah feel about hosting Nana's party?" she asked Becca after a lull in customers.

"He's excited." Becca moved some trays around in the pastry case. "It won't give him much time to get the place finished, but it's motiving."

"Have we decided what to give Nana as a gift?" Carly asked, sliding a fresh tray of brownies into the case.

"I had an idea, actually," Becca said. "Nana has always

shared her recipes with everyone here in town. What if we could return the favor?"

Jill liked the sounds of this, but she wasn't sure where her sister was going with the idea. "You mean, like a cookbook?"

Becca nodded. "Like a Hope Hollow recipe collection. We could ask everyone who knows her to share their favorite family recipe, and maybe a story that goes along with it."

"That's a wonderful idea!" Carly exclaimed. "Daisy will want to contribute, probably on behalf of Nick." She laughed because it wasn't a secret that Nick had never been good in the kitchen.

"Jonah will probably share his peach cobbler recipe," Becca said, blushing a little at his name.

"That's such a good idea that I'm surprised the town hasn't thought of it sooner," Jill said. "If enough people chip in, it could be a real treasure for the town. Something people might even want to buy."

"You mean we could make copies?" Carly asked.

"We could do better than that." Jill thought of how important Hope Hollow was to Nana, how she always said it was the community that pulled her through the tough times in life, after losing her husband and then her daughter, their mother. It was one of the reasons that Nana had always insisted on donating whatever didn't sell each day to a worthy cause. "What if we also sold the book, here in the shop, and the proceeds went back into the community? To the youth center. Or the animal shelter. Or the fire station."

Carly's eyes lit up at the prospect of helping her

boyfriend's place of work. "Nick said they've been hoping to upgrade their truck."

Jill looked at Becca. "What do you think? Would Nana mind sharing her gift with the town?"

Becca shook her head, grinning. "Leave it to you, Jill, to always have the best ideas."

"Hey, I thought I held that title," Carly joked.

"You do," Jill told her, meaning it. It was Carly who pulled this bakery out of its rut with her fresh new recipes after Jill had been unwilling to deviate from their grandmother's ways following her retirement. If Carly hadn't come back... Jill still felt tense just thinking of how close they'd been to losing this bakery.

"We can put a sign on the counter," Carly suggested.

Jill nodded. "Anyone who wants to contribute can, but I think we should personally reach out to those individuals who are special to Nana."

"Definitely," Becca agreed. "I'll make a list, though it will be pretty extensive."

It would be. Jill had always known that the bakery was the heart of the town, but it wasn't until Nana retired that she realized why. People weren't just stopping in for a cookie or a slice of pie. They were coming in for something that only Nana could offer them.

Jill took a steadying breath, reminding herself that she and her sisters had managed to make this bakery their own.

"Nana's given so much to the people in town. I bet everyone will want to give back in return," Carly said.

"We'll divide and conquer then," Jill said. "I don't mind knocking on doors, especially since I'll be taking more walks now."

Again her heart swelled at the thought of her little guy, waiting for her at home. For the first time in a long time, she glanced at the clock, eager for the day to be over.

"Good thing it's my turn to close up tonight," Becca said.

"And I can take tomorrow night," Carly added. "For the next few weeks at least, we've got things covered."

"Oh." Jill felt her anxiety kick in. She wasn't used to not overseeing the prep, at least for the majority of the time.

"No arguing," Becca warned. "We're equal partners in this business, meaning you have just as much right to time off as we do."

"Yes, but it hardly seems fair..."

"Fair?" Becca raised an eyebrow. "You close up five days out of six, and you often come in on Wednesdays when we're closed."

"We're not taking no for an answer," Carly agreed firmly. "Consider this payback for all the nights you let us go have our fun."

Payback. It had certainly never felt sweeter.

"What would I do without you two?" Jill said, shaking her head.

"Fortunately, you'll never have to know," Carly said lightly.

Jill wanted to believe that just as much as she'd once prayed that a miracle would be found for their mother. But then she reminded herself that her sisters were here, now, together in this kitchen, and that the three of them were a team in this bakery. And for the second time in two days, her heart had never felt fuller.

27

*

Frankie couldn't hide his relief the next evening when he checked the clock in the kitchen of Concetti's and saw that he only had one hour until his shift started at the fire station. He knew that Nick and the guys liked it when he came in because he always brought trays of pasta and garlic bread with him, which beat whatever one of them was cooking for the crowd.

But tonight he had other reasons for looking forward to slipping away. His mother was in full matchmaking mode, and this time, she wasn't listening to any of his protests.

"My sister Angela told me that she knows a very nice girl who will be at the wedding," Mamma said now as she sprinkled fresh cheese over a lasagna. It was a top seller in the restaurant, even more popular than their pizzas, which was saying a lot, considering how people raved about their pizza sauce—an old recipe passed down from Frankie's father's mother and cherished by Frankie's mother in his honor.

"Angela says that she just got out of a long relationship," Mamma went on as she slid the lasagna into an oven. She looked at Frankie over her shoulder. "Says she's looking to settle down. Wasted enough time on the wrong man. I said it's a good thing we have the perfect guy right here!"

Frankie pushed out a sigh and checked the clock again. Time always seemed to slow down when his mother got like this. It would be a rough couple of weeks, like the time his cousin Enzo met his now-wife Christa, at a family birthday party that Frankie hadn't attended because he'd been at the fire station.

To hear Mamma tell it, Christa could have been his wife if things had gone differently that night. Then she'd be the one with the twin grandsons (one for each knee!) instead of Angela.

But even that setback had eventually faded from Mamma's mind. He told himself that this too would pass.

For some reason, though, he had the sneaking suspicion that it wouldn't. That his time was up. That Mamma meant business. And she wasn't going to rest until he was asking for her diamond ring that she had told him many times she'd happily pull from her finger whenever he asked.

"I'll go check on the tables before heading out," he told her.

"Can you run a delivery for me on the way?" Mamma ladled two bowls of fresh minestrone soup into bowls for the couple who came in every week, always sat at the same table, and always ordered the same thing for as long as Frankie could remember.

"These for the Wagners?" he asked, even though he already knew the answer. He carefully picked up the tray, walked into the dining room, and set the soup bowls in front of the patient couple. They smiled their thanks before lifting their spoons, eating in silence as they usually did.

Frankie watched them for a moment before stepping back into the kitchen, trying to picture himself like this, decades down the road. His dating streak usually only lasted a few weeks at best, and he couldn't even imagine reaching a point of knowing someone so well that there was nothing left to say, but instead taking comfort in a quiet dinner, in companionable silence.

The only time he had a quiet dinner with someone lately was when Mamma was stewing over his lack of a love life. And that was far from relaxing.

Bracing himself, he pushed back through the kitchen door to see his mother popping a lid onto a large tray of pasta for everyone at the station. Two others were already waiting on the counter, along with a delivery bag.

They didn't do many runs—most people in town preferred to come in, see Mamma Maria, and enjoy the sidewalk cafe music that they piped through the speakers.

He checked the tab. Jill Parker, and just around the corner, too.

"No problem, Ma. I'll see you tomorrow," he said, gathering everything up in one armful, if only to make a quick getaway.

Mamma only clucked her tongue. "Look at those strong arms. Such a shame. Such a shame…"

*

Frankie wasn't a stranger to the small cottage around the corner from Main Street. The Sunrise Sisters had lived here for years, and while Becca and Jill usually picked up takeout after a long day at the bakery, or enjoyed a sidewalk table and a shared bottle of wine, they weren't shy in ordering a pizza either, and they knew better than to do it from a chain place in the next town over.

The Parkers, like the Concettis, appreciated good food and valued family traditions.

Frankie knocked on the front door, startled when he heard the barking of what he could assume was a very small dog from somewhere inside. Double-checking he hadn't gone to the wrong address on the street lined with small, wood-sided houses, he remembered that Nana Parker and her husband Robert Quincy had just gotten a puppy. Perhaps Nana was visiting, not that Nana Parker would ever bother with takeout from Concetti's. She liked seeing Mamma too much, and the feeling was mutual.

There was a scuffle behind the door and then a turning of the locks. Jill's face appeared first, looking more anxious than he was used to seeing it. Usually, when he saw her at the bakery or around town, she just seemed serious. Pleasant, but focused. Now, her blond hair was sliding out of its bun and her blue eyes looked a little alarmed. And as the door opened a little more he saw the reason why. A little ball of light brown fur that couldn't possibly weigh more than his shoe was wriggling with all its might against her chest.

"Sorry," she said, a little breathlessly. "He's stronger than he looks, and I'm afraid if I put him down he'll make a run for it."

She attempted to lift one hand for the bag of food but quickly returned it to the ornery dog. She gestured frantically and stepped deeper into her hallway.

Frankie stepped inside and closed the door behind him while Jill set down the dog and took the bag from him.

"Who is this little guy?" Frankie asked, crouching down. Even though he was only about five feet from where Jill had set him down, the puppy sprinted to Frankie at full speed, his eyes lit with mischief.

"I'm still working out a name," Jill said, looking

exhausted. "I just got him last night. He was so quiet then. And now..."

Frankie grinned as he petted the puppy. "Now he's comfortable." He looked up at Jill. "Means you're doing something right. He feels safe and loved."

Jill seemed to relax at that.

"Funny," Frankie said, standing up. "I never pictured you as the dog type."

She gave him a wary look. "No? What...type did I strike you as?"

He resisted saying the slightly uptight type. It was no secret in town that of all the Parker women, Jill was the most foreboding. Nice. Friendly. But no-nonsense.

"Well, dogs make a lot of mess." He looked into the adjacent living room, on full display through the wide doorway, where a sofa and chair sat around a coffee table, both covered in pristine white slipcovers.

For now.

"Why are you smiling like that?" Jill asked, narrowing her eyes. "Besides, I work at a bakery. I think I'm used to a mess."

"I'm just saying," Frankie said, all too aware of the lift of her eyebrow. "Baking is all about precision, right? Cooking is different. You just...feel what the food needs."

If he didn't know better, he'd say that her eyebrow went up another notch. "Baking is precise, but a lot of love goes into our recipes at the bakery. Besides, I don't see what this has to do with me having a puppy."

"It's a lot of work," he explained, realizing now that he never should have said anything.

"You think I don't know the meaning of hard work?" she countered.

"I just meant that a puppy…it requires a level of…flexibility." He braced himself as the silence stretched, even the little furball seemed to be watching Jill, waiting for her reaction. In order to see her he had to pull his head all the way back, as if he were staring up at the ceiling.

But suddenly Jill laughed. The puppy barked. And Frankie felt his shoulders sink with relief.

"Is this why you're ordering takeout instead of stopping by the restaurant tonight?" he asked.

"That and the fact that I can't exactly go to a restaurant if I don't have anyone to dine with," she said as she rifled through her handbag on the entry table.

"Yeah, I get that. I heard that Becca moved out." He was tight with the guys in town, two of which dated and now lived with Jill's sisters. "And now you have this little guy." Frankie resisted the urge to pick up the dog. He was a cute little thing.

This brought a smile to Jill's face. "Yep. Now I have him."

She handed him some bills. "Keep the change."

Frankie thanked her and pocketed the money, knowing that he'd donate the tip to the fire station. The department was underfunded and always looking for ways to improve things.

"Well, I should go, I'm on shift tonight at the station."

"Oh, before you go!" Jill set a hand to her forehead, clearly frazzled. "I almost forgot!"

Forgot? Since when did Jill Parker forget anything?

33

Even when they were kids in school together, she'd never had a late assignment. If anything, she often handed things in early.

It was annoying as heck back then. Now, he sort of admired it.

But the Jill standing before him was flush-faced and wild-haired. And the puppy was getting fidgety again. Was she even aware that the little guy was chewing on the ankle of her sweatpants?

Frankly, he was surprised that Jill would even wear something as casual as sweatpants. Sweatpants implied relaxation, something that didn't exactly match Jill's driven personality.

"We're doing a community cookbook for my grandmother's birthday," Jill started. "It started as a gift idea, but then we thought about how the entire town might like it. And how the proceeds could go to a good cause. And we thought of the fire station."

"Really?" Frankie was impressed.

"I was hoping you could give us the recipe for your famous pizza sauce. It's everyone's favorite and—" She stopped at his expression.

Frankie shook his head gravely. "No, I'm sorry. I could offer up something else, maybe. The minestrone. Our house marinara? But not the pizza sauce."

The pizza sauce at Concetti's was special, but not for the reasons that Jill knew. It wasn't about the measurements of spices or what brand of canned tomatoes they used for the base, it was about who had taught him that recipe, the one that he promised to carry on, long after his father had taken his last breath.

"But the sauce is what brings everyone to your restaurant. When people think of Concetti's, they think of the pizza sauce." Jill smiled, her eyes now hopeful.

Frankie said more firmly, "That's not something I can share."

It would be like giving away a memory, a part of himself, a moment with his father that was sacred, and cherished. He could still remember his eighth birthday when his father deemed him old enough to learn the recipe. How the man had made a big deal of standing with him beside the stove, carefully guiding him through the steps, clasping his hand on Frankie's back when he finally tasted it.

"You'll carry this on for me," he'd told Frankie that day, and Frankie hadn't thought much of it other than that one day, he'd take over the restaurant, like he always knew he would.

Now, he couldn't make that sauce without hearing his father's words in his mind. Remembering that one perfect afternoon in the kitchen.

"But the proceeds will go to the fire station," Jill tried.

"I'm sorry, Jill," Frankie said, meaning it. He didn't like to let people down, especially the Parkers, who took pride in their family business just like he did.

Jill looked disappointed as he reached for the doorknob, but she gave him a cheeky grin before he could leave. "If I ask your mother she might agree. She's always liked me, you know."

"You can try," was all Frankie said, knowing that she wouldn't. Jill might be stubborn, but she wasn't pushy.

But as he walked down the steps toward his car, he stopped for a moment to look back—into the house where that puppy was no doubt biting ankles and running amuck and giving Jill more than she'd reckoned for.

She'd said something that made his mind start to wander and an idea take form. His mother had always liked the Sunrise Sisters, hadn't she?

chapter three

The bakery was closed on Wednesdays, but that never stopped Jill from working—until today. She woke to puppy licks all over her face, which she'd quickly come to realize was better than any caffeine boost.

It was a clear day, one that promised lots of sun and long walks, and this afternoon, a visit to Nana for some puppy playtime. Jill's grandmother had called last night while Jill was enjoying her takeout with her little puppy snoring on the sofa beside her. If it hadn't been for the fact that he was sleeping so peacefully, she probably would have invited Nana and Sugar over on the spot. Instead, she and Nana had brainstormed names, and when Jill came across the name Toffee, she knew she'd found the perfect one.

After a quick breakfast, Jill attached the lead to Toffee's collar, setting out on a mission to buy a name tag, but not minding all the smiles and fawning that he received on the short walk into town.

"I see you've still got him," a deep voice called out from behind her.

Jill frowned, wondering if the person was speaking to her, and turned to see Frankie Concetti approaching with a grin.

"Of course I still have him!" Really, what made Frankie think that she wasn't up to the job? She decided to ask Frankie that the moment he was close enough that she didn't have to shout. Her frustration grew as the gleam in his eyes grew closer. "Why do you find it so strange that I have a dog?"

"Because you like neat and orderly. You're a perfectionist, Jill. It's not an insult." He shrugged his broad shoulders, his dark gaze not conveying any malice.

But then, of course, they didn't. Frankie might be one for practical jokes, but he was a decent guy, a family guy, one who had been "raised right" as Nana liked to say.

Still, she couldn't help but feel stung by his words, even if he didn't intend for them to hurt, and even if she knew that they were true. She did like her routine, her schedule, and for life to go as planned. Losing her mother as a teenager had made her all too aware of how uncertain life could be, and where she could avoid that feeling, she did.

"Well, it certainly feels like one," Jill replied.

"Come on, Jill," Frankie said casually. "You know yourself. And I've known you all my life."

Jill conceded with a nod. "I admit, I like structure."

"Nothing wrong with that. As long as you're open to life's little surprises." Frankie motioned to Toffee, who was looking around the street with wide eyes and a wagging tail. "And from the looks of it, you are."

"And are *you* open to surprises?" Jill countered.

"Absolutely!" Frankie laughed. "I'm looking at one!"

Jill narrowed her eyes but she couldn't stay mad at Frankie for long. Growing up, he'd always been a nice guy, loyal to his mother, especially after his father passed, and a hard worker, too—no one ever heard Frankie complain. But everyone heard Mamma Maria complain, especially as the years went on and Frankie was still playing the dating field. For something that bothered his mother so greatly, Frankie didn't seem fazed.

But then, that was Frankie. He didn't get bogged down by emotions or take anything too seriously.

Except maybe that family recipe.

"Have you given any more thought to the community cookbook?" she asked.

He tipped his head. "This is important to you."

"Of course it is!" She pulled Toffee's leash a little tighter as some people passed by. "It's a big birthday for my grandmother, not that she'd ever admit it. We want to make it special for her. This town means so much to her, and I know a part of her misses being at the bakery every day, serving her recipes to her friends."

Frankie grew quiet. "I understand. My mother loves nothing more than feeding everyone who comes into Concetti's. To her, each person who enjoys her food is family."

"And so is this community," Jill pressed. "You know it as well as I do, Frankie. The people in this town have supported our families. And not just their businesses."

Frankie's jaw tensed, and for a moment, Jill worried that she'd said too much. Some wounds, she knew, could never be healed, and Frankie had lost his father not long before her mother had passed away. Concetti's wasn't just a restaurant. It was a namesake.

"Mamma's never happier than when we have a full dining room," Frankie said.

"And you want Mamma Maria to be happy, don't you?"

Frankie's eyes seemed to glint, and for a second, Jill's chest swelled with hope, but all too quickly, he heaved a sigh.

"I wish I could help you—" Frankie started to say, then, seeing her disappointment, he gave her a funny look. He seemed to pause before he spoke again, like he was weighing a decision. "I'll tell you what. I'll give you the recipe for the sauce if you do something for me in return."

"Name it!" Jill said quickly, her heart leaping. She hadn't expected this, but then, she hadn't expected any of the things that had happened this week.

"Go out with me," Frankie said simply.

Jill stared at him, wondering if she'd misheard, or if this was his idea of a joke and if she was supposed to laugh, because as Frankie had said himself, they had known each other for their entire lives and never once had he shown the slightest bit of interest in her before.

She stared into his deep-set eyes, framed by enviably long lashes, down the slope of his strong nose, and down to his full mouth, waiting for a smile to stretch that squared jaw—for his big, loud laugh to echo down the street.

Instead, he held up a hand and said, "Or…pretend to, at least."

"*Pretend?*"

Her cheeks grew hot with humiliation and anger that she had even entertained that he might be serious. Joking was one thing. But expecting her to pretend to date him was far from funny.

"Hear me out," he said quickly, clearly realizing that she was very close to walking away. "It's Mamma. She's trying to set me up with any available woman under the age of thirty-five in a five-hundred-mile radius."

"And you think that by pretending to date me, she'll stop?" Jill shook her head. "Sorry, Frankie, but I like your mother. I can't lie to her."

"We wouldn't be lying," he insisted, his eyes taking on a pleading look as he reached forward and set a strong, warm hand on her wrist, stopping her from walking away, which was exactly what she should do. "We're friends, aren't we? So let her think we're a little more than friends. For one night," he added.

"Just one night?" Jill couldn't even believe that she was continuing this conversation. Her question was more out of curiosity than actual interest. She didn't know what was more preposterous: pretending to have romantic feelings for Frankie or daring to deceive Mamma Maria.

"Just for my cousin's wedding. Two weeks from Saturday. After that, we'll go back to just being friends."

"We *are* just friends," Jill reminded him. Which was exactly why she should have known he wouldn't actually ask her out, or even joke about it.

He gave her a devilish lift of one eyebrow. "Yes, but Mamma doesn't need to know that."

Jill gaped at him and then shook her head. "You're crazy."

"So you won't do it? Even for a friend?"

"Even for a friend," she said firmly as she continued on her walk. Frankie, however, was matching her stride for stride.

"Even for the sauce?" He gave her a knowing look when she stopped walking and stared at him.

"Yesterday you wouldn't even consider giving me that recipe and now you're willing to do it in exchange for…this?" She couldn't even repeat the details of his ridiculous plan. "Why are you suddenly so willing to hand it over?"

"I'm far from willing," he said, his expression turning serious. "But it was something you said…about this town. About what it means to your grandmother, and my mother. And to me. And…to my father."

She released a pent-up sigh, her frustration fading into one of understanding.

"I wouldn't be asking for that specific recipe if it wasn't so special. And this cookbook isn't just for Nana. It's for everyone who supported her. And in turn, it will support them."

Frankie nodded. "I'm not arguing that it isn't a good cause. It's a fantastic idea, really."

"Just not one you can support without a bit of bribery?" She folded her arms across her chest.

Frankie looked down at the ground for a moment, and when he looked up again, she saw the struggle on his face. "It's the other thing you said, about wanting to make my mother happy. It's not easy for me to part with that recipe, Jill, but if it means I can somehow make Mamma happy then…maybe it will be worth it."

Now Jill hesitated, thinking that everyone in town would be wanting to contribute their most special recipe to the collection, and that everyone, especially Nana, would be eagerly anticipating Concetti's pizza sauce to be included, highlighted, even.

But then she thought of Maria Concetti, the bubbly, warm woman who had brought them dinner every night for a month after Jill's mother had died. Who had been like a second daughter to Nana, more than a neighbor or a fellow shop owner.

Maria wanted nothing more than to see Frankie settled, married, preferably with kids. But it was more than that, Jill knew. She wanted to see Frankie loved. Nothing would bring her more joy.

And Jill couldn't get her hopes up like that.

"No deal," Jill said, shaking her head as she started to walk away.

She had her limits. And even pretending to date Frankie of all people was pushing things too far.

*

Jill was still thinking about Frankie's offer three hours later, alternating between amusement and anger at the audacity of such a ludicrous suggestion! It was bribery. Or blackmail. Or something altogether nefarious. She'd gotten used to Frankie's joking over time, he was known for it during their school years, but they were grown adults now and this was far from funny.

Besides, who would even believe it? They'd traveled in the same social circle for years, had mutual professional

43

respect, and up until this point had never given each other a second glance.

And did he expect her to lie to her sisters, too? For them to lie to their significant others, who were good friends with him and had been for years? And what about Nana?

Jill picked up the lemonade that was warming in the sun and took a long sip. In the yard, Sugar and Toffee were chasing each other within the confines of Nana's fenced-in yard. Jill was on watch duty while her sisters and Nana carried lunch out to the patio table.

"I still can't believe you have a dog!" Carly said happily as she set down a plate of sandwiches.

"Why does everyone keep saying that?" Jill asked her.

Carly gave the question brief consideration and then shrugged. "I guess you never mentioned wanting one before, at least not since we were kids. It's just so spontaneous for you."

In other words, she was echoing everything that Frankie had said, an opinion many shared, it would seem.

"Well, someone in the family has to think things through," Jill teased, knowing that Carly wouldn't take offense. They'd fallen into their roles naturally, maybe by birth order, or maybe by personality, or maybe one impacted the other. Jill had always been the responsible sister, and that had allowed Carly to be more carefree.

Sometimes, Jill envied her youngest sister for the freedom she had, and even though Carly liked to point out that it wasn't hers alone, it often felt that way. When Carly moved away for college and then stayed away for ten years, Jill had remained behind, because they couldn't all run off, living where they pleased, could they? Not when Nana needed help at the bakery. And especially not when her arthritis forced her to finally retire.

Jill watched Becca emerge from the screen door, knowing that her middle sister shared this sense of obligation to the family, even though neither would consider it a burden. It was a calling, a legacy, and one that they were proud to carry on.

Her sisters might claim that Jill took the bakery too seriously, but Becca had been the one to stay behind when her then-fiancé got a job opportunity in California. For a while, they'd all thought she'd lost her true love. But love found a way, didn't it?

Jill looked back toward the yard now, where the puppies were lounging in the shade of Nana's maple tree, tongues out, taking a much-needed rest from all their play.

Yes, love found a way. Sometimes it just took a little longer than you wanted it to. But patience was something she'd learned at an early age, baking in the kitchen with her mother and grandmother. You couldn't rush good things.

And now look at Becca, back together with Jonah, Carly reunited with Nick Sutton, and Nana remarried to her former next-door neighbor, Robert Quincy.

And Jill. Still single.

But no longer alone.

"It's a good thing I didn't make the leftovers run the other night," Becca said as looked fondly across the yard and settled into a seat beside Jill. "I'm not sure what Jonah would have said if I'd come home with a puppy. He's so busy setting up the new restaurant."

"Nana, did Becca tell you her idea?" Jill glanced at her sister for approval and received a nod. "We were thinking of holding your celebration at Jonah's new restaurant!"

Nana looked pleased even when she tried to hide it. "Well, if it gives Jonah a good excuse to bring in a crowd, then a party it is."

Carly gave both of her sisters a knowing grin across the table. Nana was probably already planning her outfit or would do it as soon as they left.

"But my birthday is three and a half weeks away," Nana went on, turning to Becca. "Will Jonah be ready in time?"

Becca sipped her lemonade and then nodded. "This has certainly given him some extra motivation, but yes, I think so. Of course, he'll be ironing out the little details for weeks if not months after he officially opens."

"Brings me back to my early days at the bakery," Nana said wistfully.

"We could hold it there!" Becca said, but Nana brushed aside her concern.

"I've spent plenty of birthdays in the bakery. It's important to me to support Jonah, especially now that he's family."

Jill exchanged a small smile with Becca. It was still a running joke that their grandmother had married Jonah's grandfather, even if it was the catalyst for Becca and him reuniting.

"And you know how much I love supporting other businesses. Community is important to me," Nana added.

"I can help you with the guest list, Nana," Carly volunteered. Then, turning to Jill she said suggestively, "Maybe I can add some eligible men to it."

Olivia Miles

"It wasn't so long ago that you were single," Jill reminded her. "And you," she added to Becca. "It's a family party. Why should I worry about showing up alone like I always do?"

"Because you said it yourself," Carly said. "You always do."

It was true, Jill always did show up alone. It had never really bothered her...until recently.

She thought about what Frankie had said about his cousin's wedding, wondering if this was how he felt when Mamma Maria started getting notions. If he was growing tired of seeing everyone else paired off, or if, like her, it only drew attention to his single status.

Shaking away any thoughts of Frankie's schemes or Carly's matchmaking efforts, Jill focused on defending herself.

"Besides, I have a new puppy—"

"Exactly," Carly said, looking at her frankly. "It's okay to admit that you want more in your life. You don't have to be shy with us. We're your family."

Her rather nosy and intrusive family, at least of late.

Jill brushed aside her sister's words and plated some fruit salad. "Have you ever known me to be shy?"

Becca raised her hand. "Don't you remember our high school dances?" She looked at Jill guiltily. "You would always disappear to the bathroom claiming you had a problem with your dress, but I knew it was because you were worried that no one would ask you to dance."

Or more like she was worried that someone would ask her to dance. She was still reeling from the loss of her

47

mother back then, still getting through each day in survival mode. She couldn't open her broken heart—not when she was too busy trying to piece it back together.

"That was like fifteen years ago," she told Becca with a shake of the head.

"Hiding out in the bakery kitchen isn't much different than the school bathroom," Carly said with an eyebrow lift.

"I admit that I could get out more," Jill said, hoping that would silence her sisters.

"You've already taken the first step!" Becca gave her a smile of encouragement.

"You meet so many people walking a dog!" Nana's eyes went wide.

You could say that again, Jill thought. She'd already seen just in one morning how many people were eager to stop and chat, ask her Toffee's name, and old he was. But she knew that this wasn't what Nana was implying.

"It's such an easy conversation starter," Nana continued. "They ask about the dog, then they ask about you, and you ask about them, and before you know it, you've found a new friend."

"Or more than a friend." Carly waggled her eyebrows.

"Since when are you all so concerned about my love life?" Jill asked the table, growing exasperated.

"Since we've all realized how much more there is to life than the bakery," Nana replied, and Becca nodded in agreement.

"And since you've shown us that deep down you do want more in your life," Carly said as Toffee walked over to the table and nuzzled at Jill's leg.

Olivia Miles

Wanting more and actually having it were two very different things, but Jill didn't want to continue this conversation by saying as much.

Looking down into Toffee's big brown eyes she sighed. Maybe now that she had him, her family would stop pushing her to put herself out there.

Or maybe…

Maybe she could go along with Frankie's ridiculous ruse—if it meant she could include the pizza sauce recipe in the community cookbook.

And if it meant her family might stop playing matchmaker for a while.

49

chapter four

By the next afternoon, Jill couldn't tear her eyes from the couple near the window, and not just because they had been occupying one of the best tables in the bakery for the better part of two hours. It was getting late, Carly was already wiping down surfaces, and there hadn't been anything baking in the kitchen since lunchtime.

But there was something else about the couple that drew Jill's attention. They were about her age, probably tourists, both wearing wedding rings, both completely at peace with a quiet afternoon, a shared slice of pie, and two good cups of coffee.

That made love look so easy. But she knew that it was rarely, if ever, so simple.

"I'd have expected you to be gone by now," Becca said, coming in through the kitchen and interrupting Jill's thoughts.

Jill pushed her focus onto her sister. She knew that both Becca and Carly had promised to take turns closing up for the next few weeks, but she also knew that they had personal lives, and she wasn't the only one with someone waiting for her at home.

"Carly's closing up tonight," Becca told her, reading the worry on her face. "Daisy should be coming in soon to help. She's apparently been talking about it ever since Carly told her the plan. You know she'll probably end up running this place someday."

Jill smiled at that. Not long ago, she didn't like to imagine what would come of this place in thirty years, especially when Nana had a "family only" policy and Jill didn't like to stray too far from traditions. But now there was hope for a new generation—even if it might not come from her.

"I can do the drop-off tonight," Jill offered, knowing that Becca might not say it, but she probably wanted to see how Jonah's restaurant was coming along before it got too late. "It's a beautiful day and I can take Toffee along for the walk."

There would be about a dozen assorted pastries to take to the fire station—their usual Thursday visit when there were leftovers.

"I'm sure everyone at the station will be thrilled by the visit," Carly said, approaching the counter with a stack of plates she'd cleared. "Nick can't wait to see that puppy. But Daisy will be mighty jealous."

"How about you and Daisy swing by my place after you're done here then?" Jill took a white box from the stack they kept under the counter and began filling it with muffins, brownies, cookies, and a few slices of cake that she knew would go fast.

"I'd better text Nick and tell him to save a little room for dessert," Carly said, inspecting the contents before Jill sealed the box. "He tends to overserve himself whenever Frankie's on shift."

"Frankie's at the station tonight?" Jill tried to keep her tone light, but she struggled to make eye contact with either of her sisters.

Neither of them seemed to pick up on anything, but then, Jill wasn't sure why they would. Frankie was a pal, a regular face in their lives, someone they'd all come to rely on when Mamma Maria told him to lend a hand. It had been Frankie who had moved extra tables and chairs from Concetti's storage room to their storefront when the sisters were reconfiguring their seating area before they decided to embark on a minor renovation. And it was Frankie who had personally carried Nana's wedding cake from the bakery kitchen to Concetti's party room for Nana's wedding reception. He was reliable. Happy to help.

And now, he was calling in a favor.

Jill tried to push away the thought, but even after she'd left the bakery and driven home, she still couldn't completely succeed. It had been on her mind far too much, creeping in here and there, ever since her lunch at Nana's yesterday afternoon. Pretending to date Frankie would go a long way in keeping her family from pestering her about her love life, at least for a little while.

Wait. Was she really considering this?

She jammed her key into her front door, sparking a

wave of eager barking from the back of the house. Setting the bakery box on the console table where curious paws couldn't reach it, she hurried back to the laundry room to see Toffee looking up at her, every toy in his box scattered in the small space, his bed overturned, and a look of pure joy in his round eyes.

"You've been busy today," Jill remarked, scooping him up and enjoying the lick he gave her cheek. "Guess that makes two of us."

And the day still wasn't over. She attached his lead and, grabbing the bakery box, she went back outside. The sun was still bright, but dropping in the sky, and around the corner, Main Street was coming alive, with people closing up shops for the day, and others out for an early dinner, wanting to jumpstart the weekend. The fire station was in the opposite direction, not far from town, but closer to Jill's grandmother's house. She'd probably have just enough time to walk there and back before Carly and Daisy stopped over. Normally, Jill would be sure to have ice cream in the freezer for Daisy, but today she guessed that Daisy wouldn't have any interest in dessert, only playtime.

The walk, however, took a little longer than it normally would, not only because Toffee's little legs couldn't carry him as quickly as Jill's long strides. Every couple and mother and child that walked by stopped to marvel at Toffee, ask his name, and if they could pet him. And how could Jill say no?

By the time she arrived at the station, she expected Toffee to be ready for a nap, but the wag of his tail told her otherwise. At least he'd sleep well tonight.

That made one of them, Jill thought, her stomach swooping when the first person she saw as she approached the glass door of the station was none other than Frankie Concetti, carrying a stack of food cartons to the large dining table.

She looped the leash around her wrist to knock, hoping that Nick or even Zach might notice her first, but Frankie was closest, and after a slight pause, his mouth lifted into a grin.

At least they were still on speaking terms, she thought. But then, Frankie was good-natured, always friendly, like an extension of the family. Maybe that was why he'd felt comfortable asking her to help him out. But was she comfortable saying yes?

"You still have the puppy!" he said when he opened the door, and the wink he tossed her told her that, this time, he was joking.

"And he has a name now," she informed Frankie. "This is Toffee."

"Toffee." Frankie mulled it over. "It suits him."

Jill smiled. "I thought so too." Handing him the bakery box, she said, "Leftovers. I hope there's enough to go around."

"If I don't eat them all first." Frankie's eyes grew when he popped the lid and sneaked a peek.

"Don't you get enough dessert at your restaurant?" Jill remarked, knowing that the Concettis were strong supporters of the bakery but Mamma Maria still prided herself on the best cannoli—something that the Parkers had never dared to make.

"Not like this," Frankie replied, setting the box on the table.

Jill nodded, knowing that she was free to go. Her errand had been run and food delivered. Toffee would be getting hungry soon, and they still had the walk home.

But something in Frankie's eyes made her hesitate. Along with the nagging thought that if she didn't say something now, she'd just end up thinking about it the entire walk home. And maybe tomorrow too.

In other words, best to get it over with.

"I've been thinking about what you said." She gave him a suggestive look, hoping that she didn't have to say anymore out loud. Frankie's head tipped with interest. Or maybe surprise. "Were you serious about that?"

"Why? Are you up for it?" His dark eyes gleamed and for a moment she wondered if he was having some fun with her, the way he used to do back in school when she'd spend all weekend studying for a test, feeling very prepared, and he'd tell her that the quiz wasn't until Friday just to watch her eyes widen in horror.

She'd fallen for his pranks enough times to be wary.

"That depends," she said, not yet willing to show her hand, not until she knew more details. "How do you see this playing out?"

Frankie glanced behind him as a bunch of guys came into the room, wasting no time in helping themselves to plates and piling each one with mounds of pasta. Nick held up his hand and Jill gave a friendly wave.

"Why don't you meet me at the Rustic Tavern tomorrow night and we can talk about it then?" Frankie suggested.

Jill glanced around the room. They were hardly alone, but she also needed to know what he was implying before she agreed to anything.

"I didn't say I was on board with this yet," she whispered.

"Relax, Jill." He gave a little chuckle. "I'm just suggesting a drink on a Friday night. It's not a big deal."

Maybe not to him, considering how often he dated, but to her, it was a very big deal. She frequented the bar often enough, but usually with her sisters, and lately, with their significant others. Sometimes Frankie was there too, and Zach, another firefighter. Often Carly's friend Joanna joined, or members of Becca's book club. Most of Jill's friends from school had been married for years by now, many with children that kept them home at night.

"Unless…you'd prefer to meet somewhere more private?" Frankie asked, sensing her hesitation.

"No," she blurted. No, absolutely not. The last thing she'd ever even considered was a little alone time with Frankie Concetti. The guy was a chum. Not quite a brother, but more like a cousin. "The tavern will be fine."

She couldn't believe she'd agreed to this, and only because he'd all but called her bluff, implied that she couldn't handle it, that it was too much for her—even if it was.

When was the last time she'd sat with any guy, for a drink, without the company of at least Becca? So long ago, that she couldn't even remember. And even then, it had been an unmemorable, stilted conversation over a glass of wine or coffee, a vague mention of a call that would never be made.

This was Frankie. Mamma Maria's son. Childhood schoolmate. It wasn't a big deal to him and it shouldn't be a big deal to her.

But as she walked back out onto the street with Toffee nipping at her heels, her stomach stirred uneasily.

She had plans for a Friday night, and ones that didn't include a remote control or takeout or a bottle of wine with her sisters. She was stepping outside of her comfort zone—for the second time in one week.

And as she smiled down at her sweet little dog, she had a feeling that this time around she might be pushing her luck.

*

Jill was so busy raiding her closet that she hadn't even heard her sister knock until Carly's voice called out her name from the front hall, sounding just a little worried.

"Carly?" Jill pulled another decade-old sundress from a hanger and tossed it over her shoulder. "I'm upstairs in my bedroom!"

To that, Toffee gave two squeaky barks, as if to say that he, too, was upstairs.

Jill heard the pounding of feet on the floorboards followed by silence. Carly stood in the open doorway of her bedroom, her eyes wide. Daisy clamped a hand over her mouth to cover her giggles, with little success.

"Spring cleaning?" Carly asked, knowing full well that it was the end of summer.

"Where's the puppy?" Daisy asked excitedly, getting right to the purpose of this visit.

"He was just here." Jill looked around the bedroom, which had gone from immaculate and obsessively organized to having the bed, and nearly the entire floor, strewn with old clothing that even she knew was no longer in style.

"Toffee?" she cried out, feeling the panic seize her chest. He'd just been here a minute ago—surely she would have noticed if he'd slipped out of the room?

"There he is!" Daisy cried, pointing to a pile of old, faded tee shirts that should be moved to the rag bin.

At the sound of his name, the clothes wiggled, and a moment later, his furry little face popped free through the neck of a faded pink tee shirt, which he then slid out of to run full speed at Daisy, who'd fallen right to her knees to greet him.

"Love at first sight," Carly commented.

"I know the feeling." Jill felt her smile go straight to her heart.

"Can I take him on a walk?" Daisy asked eagerly.

Jill looked around the room, which would have to be dealt with before she went to bed tonight, and certainly by tomorrow, when she'd have to put together something decent to wear to her...meeting. Yes, that's what it was. A meeting. A get-together. Nothing strange about it.

"You can give him a treat if you'd like," Jill offered. She was getting the impression that Carly was waiting until Daisy left the room to have her say. "There's a bag on the kitchen counter. And he likes playing tug with his rope toy, too. But gently," Jill added.

"Yes, Mom," Carly bantered, sliding Jill a knowing smile. When Daisy ran off with the puppy, Carly closed the door partway behind her. "You're good at this, you know."

"Cleaning?" Jill joked.

"Taking care of your puppy," Carly clarified. "But then, I shouldn't be surprised. You did a good job taking care of me when I was growing up."

Jill looked at her youngest sister, finding it difficult not to see her as the wide-eyed child who liked to eat more cookie batter than she could help make. The one whose light brown hair Jill would braid every day for school in the weeks after their mother had died—trying so hard to make the two sides even, to keep at least one thing consistent for the little girl when so much had changed.

Even though they'd had their differences over the years, and even when Jill had struggled not to resent Carly at times for going off in search of other interests instead of staying back in the bakery as she and Becca always had, she also admired the woman that her sister had become.

"You should talk. Look at how good you are with Daisy," Jill said fondly. "She clearly adores you."

"Well, the feeling is mutual. And Daisy's easy to love."

"So is Toffee," Jill agreed. She hoped that sent a clear message to her sister that welcoming an adorable puppy into her life was much easier than opening her heart to a romantic prospect.

Luckily, Carly had other things on her mind at the moment than Jill's love life. She motioned to the room. "So, are you going to tell me what's going on in here?"

Jill gave a casual shrug. "I was just going through my clothes. Out with the old and in with the new type of thing."

"Since when do you care how you dress?" Carly asked,

tipping her head. "No offense, Jill, but you wore that same cotton sundress you have on now twice last week and at least three times the week before. And I think you owned it before I went to college."

Jill balked, but she couldn't argue. She did wear this particular dress a lot. "It's comfortable. And it's presentable. That makes it an excellent option for work. Plus, since it is, in fact, as old as you say it is, I don't worry about getting stains on it."

Now Carly laughed. "Let me guess. It also washes well?"

"How'd you know?" Jill asked.

"Because it used to be navy, and now it's grey." Carly gave her a pointed look.

Jill looked down at the cotton sundress, realizing that her sister was right. "You have a really good memory."

"We all do, how else could we retain all those recipes that Nana and Mom taught us?"

Carly's smile turned a little sad and Jill felt the familiar ache creep into her chest. All she had left of her mother now were those recipes—and that bakery. And she'd come far too close to losing them both not too long ago.

She knew that her mother would be proud, knowing that together, with Carly's help, they had found a way to bring the bakery into the next generation, but some days, Jill couldn't help feeling like she'd almost let her mother down in the worst possible way.

She sat down on her bed, feeling exhausted from her efforts and knowing that she hadn't even solved her problem. "I think I need to go shopping."

In other words, an activity that she rarely made time for and certainly couldn't squeeze in now.

"Oh, I can go with you, this weekend!" Carly said excitedly.

"I was hoping to find something before tomorrow night," Jill lamented.

Carly pushed a few hangers to the side in the closet, inspecting each garment before moving on to the next, clearly not liking what she saw. She glanced over her shoulder. "What's so special about tomorrow?"

Jill waved a hand through the air but her heart sped up. She'd always been a rule monger, honest to a fault to hear some—like Carly, or even Frankie—tell it. It wasn't easy to omit the truth from her sister, but if she told Carly that she was meeting Frankie, her sister would get too excited, and if she told her the reason why... Well, she couldn't imagine what Carly would say to that. She just knew that Carly wouldn't approve. And it would be just one more thing that Jill would have to hear about next time they all gathered at Nana's.

"Nothing, nothing. I mean, Friday night..." Jill struggled to look at her sister.

Carly's eyes narrowed in suspicion. "Since when do you care about Friday nights? You usually like to stay in, since Saturday mornings are so busy at the bakery."

Jill chewed on her lip. If Carly was trying to drag the truth from her, she was doing a very sly job of it, and from the gleam in her sister's gaze, it was becoming increasingly clear that she was doing just that.

"Unless you have special plans that I don't know

61

about?" Carly looked at her pertly. From the silence that settled over the room, Jill knew that Carly could be patient until an answer was delivered.

"I might have drinks with a friend, that's all."

"Oh." Carly considered this. "And were you thinking that maybe it's time to put a little more effort into your appearance in case an eligible man happens to catch your attention?"

"Well, as much as I hate to admit it, you and Nana did make some good points yesterday," Jill admitted. Enough to make her consider going along with this scheme.

Carly's smile was one of satisfaction. "I knew I'd wear you down. Okay, let me see what we have to work with here, and I can always bring you my cute navy sundress tomorrow. You know, as in the one that is still navy." She picked up a cardigan from a pile and wrinkled her nose. "I can bring you some makeup samples, too. It's a good thing you have such classical features, Jill, since I've never seen you in much more than lip gloss."

"Are you trying to compliment me?" Jill snorted.

Carly turned to her, her hazel eyes wide with innocence. "Of course I am! But if you look this pretty in a ratty old dress, imagine how you can feel in something new and flirty, with a little…blush on your cheeks. And maybe a smidgen of eye shadow. And, unless you're Frankie Concetti, everyone benefits from mascara."

Jill felt her cheeks burn and she was grateful that Carly had turned back to flicking through her closet.

"Frankie does have nice eyelashes," she commented, even if she'd only just noticed them in the past few days.

62

They'd always been there, of course, but so had he. And she just hadn't had a reason to pay attention before.

"He sure does. And Maria likes reminding everyone, too."

Now they both shared a laugh.

"Thanks," Jill said, meaning it.

"No thanks needed!" Carly was clearly enjoying this more than Jill. "This will be fun."

Fun had never been a word Jill used to describe her free time or her life in general, but now, as Carly started talking about shoes and hairstyles, Jill had to admit, that maybe this wasn't a terrible idea.

Or so she hoped.

chapter five

By the next morning, Jill had already formulated an excuse to cancel on Frankie.

Her puppy was the most obvious choice—even though she did take frequent breaks from the bakery to walk him and a drink at the tavern would take an hour tops, thirty minutes if she was quick.

But that would mean that she was entertaining this idea of fake dating, and she wasn't. She was feeling guilty because Frankie had always been so good to them. And he'd caught her in a moment of weakness when her family was making her single status forefront in her mind.

She decided to say that she had to stay late at the bakery and prep. But then, that might not stop him from showing up here, considering Concetti's was just a few storefronts up the street. And if she said she had to stay home with Toffee, there was nothing to say that Frankie wouldn't invite himself over. Maybe with some takeout from the restaurant.

Then what could have been a short drink would turn into a long meal. No, that wasn't a solution.

She was starting to think of what believable ailment she could come down with in the next eight hours when the kitchen door swung open and Carly appeared, carrying a shopping bag stuffed with clothing.

"Here's that dress I promised you," Carly said, fishing it out from the top of the bag. "Amongst some other clothes and shoes you might like. And there's some makeup in there too. Unused. Samples. Not my color."

Becca set down her wooden spoon and looked on with an air of confusion. "What's this? Makeup? For you, Jill?"

"Is it that shocking?" Jill asked, her defenses rising. She took the bag and glanced inside. "I was thinking that I might want to wear something special…for Nana's birthday."

There. That was a believable excuse, and not a complete mistruth either.

But then Carly tipped her head and said, "I thought it was because you were going out with a friend tonight."

"Oh, I….have to cancel. I need to get home to Toffee." Jill smiled to herself and went back to making a coffee cake. Nana was right about a dog being a great excuse to meet people, but she'd overlooked that it was also a great excuse to stay home.

"Nick and I are staying in tonight. Why don't you let us watch him for a bit?" Carly offered. She finished tying her apron strings and met Jill and Becca around the big workbench. "Daisy would be thrilled. She didn't stop talking about Toffee the entire way home. I have a feeling I know what she'll be asking for when her birthday comes around."

"Which friend are you meeting?" Becca asked.

Maybe it was because she knew the secret she was harboring, but Jill had the distinct impression that Becca's question wasn't merely conversational.

Now, realizing that she had no excuse to cancel, not because Frankie wouldn't accept it but now Carly wouldn't either, Jill heaved a sigh, cracked an egg into her bowl, and all but whispered. "Frankie."

The kitchen went silent until Carly blurted, "Frankie Concetti?"

"Is there another Frankie?" Jill should have known she'd be met with this reaction. She wasn't just meeting a friend, she was meeting a friend of the opposite sex, alone, and that was sure to raise interest.

"But…why?" Becca blinked at her in confusion.

"He needs some advice," Jill said. There—that wasn't too far from the truth. "Something to do with his mother. A family wedding. I don't really know. I bumped into him walking Toffee and it was hard to talk. So…"

Carly nodded along, but her hazel eyes gleamed. "So it makes sense to meet for a drink. On a Friday night. Just the two of you."

"It's not like that!" Jill insisted.

Carly gave a less-than-subtle glance to Becca and then began measuring out some dry ingredients for the cinnamon chip scones. "If you say so."

*

"Frankie!" Maria called into the kitchen as she pushed through the door, carrying a large box of the dried pasta they imported from Italy.

Only the best at Concetti's, his mother always said. Mamma Maria was a proud woman, and not just of her son.

"Let me take that, Ma." Frankie stopped stirring the sauce and quickly crossed the room to relieve his mother of the heavy box.

"You're so good to me," she said, patting his cheek.

For a moment, she looked up at him with such love on her face that he thought all that nonsense the other day had been forgotten, that maybe he wouldn't need to worry about his cousin Gia's wedding at all. But just as quickly, Mamma's eyes narrowed and she said, "The only thing you've ever done to let me down is not finding a nice girl."

And there it was.

Frankie set the box on the kitchen island and began unpacking it. "I've met plenty of nice girls, Mamma. They just weren't the right girl." None that got his heart going. None that made him long for their company, or kept his interest.

And none of them passed Mamma's test. It was unwritten, a code that he couldn't even understand. One built on instinct, perhaps. Or intuition. And it didn't take much for her lips to pinch with displeasure or her eyelids to droop with disappointment.

"Maybe you're just too picky!" his mother said now.

Frankie knew better than to say he wasn't the picky one—that it didn't matter to him when that nice girl last spring had cut her spaghetti into little pieces when he'd brought her home for dinner with Mamma. He'd found it kind of funny, but he'd also known it was the last time he'd see her, without having to look at Mamma's pinched mouth and wide eyes, so large that he could see the whites all the way around.

Instead, seeing an opportunity, he said with a grin that used to let him off the hook as a kid, "It's hard to find a woman who will live up to you."

Mamma grabbed a dish towel and swatted him with it, mumbling a few phrases in her native Italian which he barely understood. But it was clear by the gleam in her eyes that she was pleased.

"Cousin Tony should be here soon to cover the front of the house," Mamma said. "Are you at the station tonight?"

Frankie shook his head. "I'm going out with friends."

"Friends." Mamma shook her head as she took over stirring the sauce. "Those guys from the fire station all have wives or girlfriends. Don't any of them have a nice sister that they could introduce to you?"

Frankie debated telling his mother exactly who he was going to meet tonight and decided against it. There was still the possibility that Jill wouldn't go along with his plan, and making an announcement prematurely would only invite more disappointment and accusations from his matchmaking mother.

"I'll be sure to ask," he said instead, sparking a look of approval from Maria. "Either way, I don't think I'll be out too late. You know I don't like to leave you and Tony too long on Friday and Saturday nights."

"Tony is ten years older than you with three beautiful daughters and a wife. He's happy for the work. A man your age needs to get out," Maria told him. "There will be plenty of time for you to stay home once you're married."

She had a one-track mind, but Frankie could only smile. He knew that all his mother wanted was the best for him.

If only Frankie could figure out what that was. Or rather, who.

*

Jill sat at a table in the Rustic Tavern, grateful that she'd arrived early enough to scout out something discreet, tucked away in the corner, where they wouldn't be on full display for all of Hope Hollow to see. Now, as the minutes ticked by, the nerves turned to irritation as she realized that Frankie was late.

She nursed her drink—a single glass of white wine she'd been sure to pay for herself to not invite any confusion about the purpose of the night. And now, as she looked across the room, a haze of familiar faces, some more so than others, she decided to give this man exactly one more minute before—

Before what? Carly had taken Toffee to her house. And if Jill showed up now, a mere thirty minutes after handing her puppy over, Carly would know she'd been stood up and then pity her, but not before inviting her inside for dinner with Nick and Daisy, because Jill couldn't exactly disappoint Daisy by taking Toffee home so soon.

For Daisy, Jill decided to stay. Whether Frankie graced her with his presence or not.

And she was beginning to hope he wouldn't. A no-show would mean that her conscience would be cleared. She wouldn't need to give another second of her time to consider this ridiculous idea of his.

Maybe he'd changed his mind. Explain to her the next time he saw her that he was sorry, that he didn't know what he'd been thinking, asking her to pose as his wedding date, of all things! He'd be sure to joke about it someday, and it would eventually be forgotten. She would go on with her quiet routine and Frankie would find a real girlfriend to bring to the wedding.

"Jill?"

She looked up to see Frankie standing in front of her table, wearing a respectable blue button-down shirt and jeans. She realized that she was used to seeing him in a tee shirt, maybe a sweater in winter, and now her eyes grazed his freshly shaven jawline, down to the broad shoulders and strong arms that certainly came in handy when he offered to help with the heavy lifting (or Mamma Maria volunteered him) and straight up to those deep-set eyes, which seemed to look at her in wonder.

"I was sitting over near the front," he explained. "I...I didn't recognize you at first."

Now Jill felt her cheeks flush with heat and she cursed herself for not showing up in the faded cotton sundress she'd worn to work. At Carly's suggestion, she'd let her hair down today, instead of in the usual tight bun that was so practical at the bakery. She didn't have much practice with makeup—never saw much reason for anything other than a swipe of lip gloss as Carly had pointed out. Other than

Nana's wedding a couple of months ago, she hadn't had a reason for dressing up.

Until tonight.

And now, by the way that Frankie was staring at her when he dropped into his seat, she wished she hadn't.

He'd take it the wrong way, perhaps. Think this was a date.

And it wasn't. So why had she made an effort?

But then, taking in his shirt and shaven face, she realized that he had, too.

This was new territory, meeting alone, just the two of them. But surely it wasn't anything more than that.

"I see you already have a drink which means that you've denied me the honor. Don't let my mother know, please, or she'll probably spank me." Frankie flashed those dimples that used to win him a lot of attention back in high school.

Jill laughed. "I'd like to see Mamma Maria try." The woman only came up to his shoulder at best.

"Oh, believe me, she's chased me around the kitchen a few times recently." Frankie laughed, a warm, deep sound that made Jill relax.

She realized, as she sipped her wine, that she was happy she'd come out tonight. It certainly beat another night on the couch, laughing at the television, and she knew that Daisy was thrilled for a little puppy time.

"And what could you possibly have done to tick off your mother?" Jill asked, knowing how the woman glowed each time his name was mentioned.

Frankie paused to order a beer from the passing waiter

and then turned back to her. "I admit that I like to play jokes on her. She's an easy target. And deep down, she enjoys it."

"Practical jokes on your mother?" Jill tsked but she smiled to show her amusement. She knew Maria as well as she knew Frankie, and he was right that his mother enjoyed a good laugh.

"Nothing too bad," Frankie explained. "Maybe I told her that the refrigerator door had been left open and all the fish went bad. Or maybe I put a plastic spider in her coffee mug a few times. That one never gets old."

He laughed again, and, imagining Maria's reaction, Jill did too.

"So, how long were you waiting before I finally found you?" Frankie asked. "I got here ten minutes before our agreed-upon time and I never saw you walk in."

He'd arrived ten minutes early? Jill didn't know why she felt touched. Maria had simply raised him right, like Nana always said. Still, she pressed a hand to her cheeks to cool them.

"Oh, my sister Carly is watching my dog tonight, so I came over straight from meeting her. We must have just missed each other," she said blandly, rather than eluding to the fact that she'd arrived twenty minutes early with the mission of scouting out this table.

"You got a good table," he remarked. Then, with a wink, he said, "I guess you wanted to be alone with me."

"What?" Now her cheeks blazed. "No. No, I mean. This table is more discreet. More—"

She stopped when she saw the gleam in his dark eyes, the dimples that quirked as he fought off a smile.

"Now I see why your mother spanks you," she said, and then immediately regretted her words when his eyebrows shot up.

"Jill Parker. If I didn't know better, I'd say that you were flirting with me."

"Don't flatter yourself," she scoffed, waving him off. "I'm here because I said I'd be here. And as for the table, I thought it would minimize the attention."

"It's not like we've never had drinks here before," he said mildly.

"Not just the two of us." Sure, they'd hung out several times under this very roof, but always in a group. She leaned across the table and whispered, "What if people get the wrong idea about this?"

He too leaned in, until they were so close that she could practically count the dark, long lashes that framed his deep eyes, and whispered, "Would that be so bad?"

Now her eyes widened and she dropped back against her chair. "You set this up! You tricked me!"

Frankie held up his hands in a show of innocence, but there was no ignoring the light in his eyes. "I just suggested we have a drink. Whatever we decide to do after this is entirely up to you."

She stared at him, taking in his sober expression—until she realized that he was struggling to maintain it.

"You're incorrigible!" she said. Now she really could picture Mamma Maria chasing him around that kitchen.

"I'm many things, but lucky in love doesn't seem to be one of them," he said after accepting his beer from the waiter.

She saw the frankness in his expression and felt her defenses drop. "Mine either. So..."

"So." He sighed and raised his glass, toasting her to that. "My cousin Gia is getting married two weeks from tomorrow. Mamma hasn't taken the news well."

"About a wedding?" She knew from Nana's recent wedding that Maria was all too happy to host the reception and celebrate the occasion.

Frankie tipped his chin. "You'd think it was a funeral."

Jill laughed lightly and took another sip of her drink. "The death of hope that you'll find a nice girl and have a lot of babies?"

"Exactly." Frankie shook his head. "She and her sisters have put their heads together to find me a wife at this wedding."

"Can you come up with a reason to not attend?" Jill inquired.

"Skip a family event?" Frankie looked horrified, and Jill understood. Frankie wouldn't want to—and he certainly wouldn't dare.

"The last time I skipped a family event was four years ago because I was on shift at the station. My cousin Enzo met a woman named Christa there." Frankie paused. "They now have two boys."

"Let me guess?" Jill knew Mamma Maria well. The woman didn't hide her emotions. "Christa could have been your wife instead?"

Frankie slapped the table. "Exactly."

"So you have to go to the wedding." Jill saw the problem. There was no way out of it.

"And I thought if I had a date, then I wouldn't have to worry about my mother matching me up with someone." Frankie sipped his drink unhappily.

"I don't know, Frankie." Jill sat back in her chair. "I'm not sure your mother would even believe it. Why would we suddenly date now, after all this time?"

Frankie shrugged. "Why not? Friends sometimes turn into more, when the timing is right."

She stared at him, knowing better than to read anything into that comment, even as her stomach gave a nervous flutter. He did have nice eyelashes, didn't he? Enviably nice, even.

Shaking away those thoughts, she cleared her throat, getting back to practical matters. "And then what, we'd tell her we broke up?"

Jill had visions of Maria Concetti stomping over to the bakery, demanding a word, asking Jill what could be so wrong with her beloved son. Voices would be raised. Explanations ordered. It wouldn't matter if there was a packed bakery or a full audience. It could potentially create a rift in the two families that had always been so close.

"I'll tell her I called things off," Frankie reassured her, clearly reading her concerns.

"But what good would that do? Then she'll have two reasons to be upset with you: for dumping me and still being single!"

Frankie considered this for a moment while he sipped his beer. "I'll cross that bridge when I get to it. For now, I just need to get through this wedding. I've never seen my mother this worked up. Usually, when one of my cousins announces an engagement or a new baby she goes into mourning for a few days and then snaps out of it."

They shared a smile across the table.

"What about my grandmother?" Jill asked. "You can't expect me to lie to her too."

"Tell her whatever you want," Frankie said casually. "Or tell her nothing. Haven't we known each other for years? Is it so strange that you might come with me to a wedding?"

Jill considered that most of the other women in town were already spoken for and reluctantly agreed.

But that didn't mean that she consented to this scheme.

"Can I think about it?" she asked, only because she wasn't ready just yet to turn him down.

Frankie held up his big palms. "Look. It will be no different than tonight. Two friends. Enjoying an evening."

Jill nodded. Easy for Frankie to say, because he had an active social life.

Whereas for her a Friday night alone with Frankie was a big deal. A rare event. And a date—or fake date—to a big family wedding was a tall ask.

And one that she would have to explain one way or another to her family. And that might cause more problems than even she could handle.

chapter six

Even though the restaurant wasn't open until five, Frankie was often at work in Concetti's kitchen well before noon, and today was no different. He got in early, going over inventory and checking the reservation list, which left just enough room for a few walk-ins.

He knew that his mother never liked to turn away business, and not just because it kept the lights on. If someone wanted their food, she was all too happy to cook for them. If she had to seat someone in the kitchen, she would, so long as they were willing.

"Ah, there you are, Frankie!" Maria came through the door that led to the staircase and the apartment above the restaurant where Frankie had been born and raised—and lived until he finally convinced his mother that a place of his own would help his social life, and only after she'd gone through an entire box of tissues after soaking her handkerchief. For months after, she found an excuse to drop by his apartment three blocks down, usually with a tray of food, even though he'd learned to cook from the best. Most nights when he wasn't at the fire station, they still ate together at Concetti's before they opened the doors to the public, trying new recipes that they'd feature as specials, or enjoying the old favorites that made them remember another time, when they had another person sharing their table.

Frankie glanced at the photo of his father than hung on the wall near the stove and grinned. It had taken a long time to get to a point where he could remember the man with a smile, but there was still a lingering pain in his chest that Frankie knew his mother shared. When he was a boy, Mamma always assured him that his father had led a full, happy life, that he'd used his time well, and it was true. This kitchen hadn't just been filled with good food and smells, but also laughter, music, and even dancing when his father took his mother for a spin across the linoleum while the sauce simmered.

He watched as his mother tied on an apron and began gathering the ingredients for the tiramisu, not even having to measure after so many years of practice.

Every so often he felt her eyes on him, pulling his attention away from his paperwork, until finally, he set down the purchase orders and said, "Is there something you wanted to say?"

"I could ask you the same thing!" she remarked as she whipped the mascarpone. "You didn't tell me you had a date last night!"

Of course. Frankie knew that his mother had her spies all over town—friends, technically, but in Hope Hollow, everyone knew everyone and their whereabouts too. It wouldn't have gone unnoticed that he was having a drink with Jill Parker.

Not that he particularly minded. He studied his mother's face to see how she felt about this, noticing that she was struggling not to smile too broadly.

"A Sunrise Sister nonetheless!" she exclaimed, using the nickname given to the trio.

"I had a beer with Jill," was all he said.

"And she had a glass of wine," Maria said, confirming that she'd gotten the full scoop from someone. "I was disappointed to hear you only bought the girl a drink and not dinner!"

Frankie knew better than to tell his mother that Jill had purchased her own glass of wine before he'd arrived and refused his offer of another, claiming she had to get back to her dog. He would have happily stayed a little longer, and not only to convince her to attend Gia's wedding with him. He'd had a surprisingly nice time with Jill.

"It was just drinks, Mamma," Frankie said. Jill hadn't agreed to anything yet, and knowing how stubborn she could be, he wasn't sure he'd be able to wear her down. He couldn't let his mother get too excited, at least not until Jill confirmed that she'd be his date to the wedding.

"Just drinks. Just a date. Just dinner!" Maria grumbled under her breath. "Why can't it ever be more with you, Frankie?"

Frankie pushed aside the papers and heaved a sigh,

knowing his mother's question was open-ended, and often spoken. He'd start on the sauce. Let it cook low and slow through the afternoon, filling the kitchen with the smell of garlic and spices by the time they opened the doors tonight.

"Jill Parker is a pretty girl," Maria commented, clearly approving.

But then, Frankie already knew that his mother would approve of Jill. That was precisely why he'd asked her to accompany him to the wedding—that and the fact that they were friendly enough that it wouldn't be completely awkward.

"Is she?" he asked. "I never really noticed."

And he hadn't. He'd always seen Jill in that tight bun, a permanent pinch between her eyebrows for as far back as he could remember. Sure, she'd lightened up a little at her grandmother's recent wedding, held right here at Concetti's. But when the music played, she stayed seated, watching others dance, much like she'd done back at school events. When the gang all got together for drinks, she rarely came along or spent most of the evening listening rather than chiming in.

But last night had been different.

Or maybe, like he'd just said to his mother, he'd never really noticed her pretty blue eyes and wide smile before— or the way her nose wrinkled when she laughed.

"Never noticed?" Maria scoffed and then waved her hands at the framed photo of her late husband. "What am I going to do with this son of ours?"

Frankie could only shake his head. "Well, Jill and I have always only been friends—"

"Until now!" Maria's eyes flashed with satisfaction when she turned to look at him. "And you owe that girl a dinner."

Frankie pulled a pot from the rack that hung over the center kitchen island where his mother had stopped preparing tonight's dessert.

"Ask her to dinner for tonight," she said firmly. "I'll give you two the best table."

"Oh, Ma—"

But the look in her eyes told him two things.

Mamma was serious.

And he might just be in real trouble now.

*

"So, Jill." Carly turned from the pastry case where they'd all gathered to handle the morning rush. "If I'd known you had a date with Frankie Concetti last night, I would have lent you one of my better dresses."

"What's this?" Becca's eyes went round.

Jill heaved a sigh and began pulling empty trays from the case. "It wasn't a date."

"That's not what I hear," Carly said pertly. "Erika and Joanna were having drinks at the bar and they said that you and Frankie looked really cozy at a private table, tucked away from the crowd, where you couldn't be interrupted. They said that at one point, you were nearly nose to nose, both leaning in across the table!"

"And you're just waiting until now to point this out?" Jill gave her youngest sister a look of disapproval. "I imagine you've been nearly bursting all morning just waiting to bring this up."

"I was waiting to see if you'd cough up the information first," Carly said. Then, leaning in to avoid being overheard by a customer approaching to grab another napkin, she said, "Why didn't you tell us that it was a date?"

"Because it wasn't a date." Jill walked toward the kitchen door, knowing that at least one of her sisters would need to stay behind and guard the counter. She could only hope that sister would be Carly.

Instead, they both chased after her, Becca being responsible enough to stand in the partially open doorway, glancing back toward the storefront.

"You could have hinted last night when you came to pick up Toffee," Carly said, looking a little hurt. "I have to say, that if I'd known it had been a real date, I wouldn't have opened the door to you so soon. You must have only been there for a little over an hour!"

"That's because it wasn't a date!" Jill was growing exasperated. She scanned the kitchen, trying to think of what she should be baking, but for once, her mind was muddled and confused. This wasn't like her, and this wasn't good. She prided herself on organization, certainty, and having everything in order, both inside this bakery and outside of it.

"Okay, but then why were you meeting Frankie, alone, for drinks?" Becca asked, giving her a fair chance to explain.

"Because he asked." Jill tossed up her arms.

Scones. She'd make another batch of scones. Those were selling fast today.

She'd managed to silence her sisters, but all too soon

she saw them exchange a glance and she knew she had said the wrong thing.

When was the last time a man—any man—had asked her out for a drink? Too long to think about. She must have had an invisible sign that told people not to bother trying.

"Well, he asked. You went. Isn't it simple enough?" Carly finally said.

Simple. There was absolutely nothing simple about having drinks with Frankie, and not only because of the ruse they were discussing. Now she saw firsthand what it would be like to date him. If she went to his cousin's wedding as his date, more people than Maria Concetti would get the wrong impression.

"I just heard the bell over the door jingle. Can we please get back to work now?" Jill said, taking on the eldest sister role, even though she knew that they were all, in fact, equal partners in the business.

She saw Carly share an exasperated look with Becca before the two disappeared behind the door, leaving Jill to finally take a breath. If she thought having Carly pester her about her nonexistent love life was bad, having her sister try to pry details about last night out of her was almost worse.

Or worse? Jill thought about the insinuation and speculation and nodded firmly. Yes, definitely worse.

She hadn't even finished dicing the butter when Carly's head poked around the door again, a mischievous smile playing at her lips.

"Carly," Jill warned. "I don't want to hear another word about Frankie Concetti!"

Carly's cheeks were pink when she nodded. "It's going to be pretty hard for me to respect your wishes, Jill."

Jill sighed deeply and set down her knife "And why is that?"

Carly grinned. "Because he's here."

*

Frankie was here. In her place of business. In the middle of a workday.

If he wasn't here for a chocolate cream pie or today's strawberry shortcake special, then any lingering thought Jill held for going along with his scheme was off the table.

"Hello, Frankie," she said, giving him her best customer appreciation smile as she walked into the storefront and behind the counter, refusing to meet her sisters' eyes, who showed no inclination of giving her any privacy. "What can I get for you today? We have a new flavor of cookies if you'd like to try a sample." She pushed the tray containing bite-sized samples toward him. To her sisters, she said, "And we have some scones that need to go into the oven if you don't mind?"

With great reluctance, Carly stepped aside. Jill waited until both of her sisters were tucked safely away in the kitchen before turning back to Frankie.

"So, what will it be? Some cookies to bring back to Mamma?"

"Actually, I was hoping to talk to you about something else," he said, looking a little nervous.

Jill glanced at the kitchen door, which only then closed completely. No doubt Carly was searching for a glass to press against it now.

"If you're here to talk about last night," Jill began in a near whisper, "this isn't a good time."

No time was a good time to discuss last night. There never should have been a last night, seeing how today was turning out. Wasn't he the one who said it would just be drinks, that she was overreacting by making a bigger deal out of it?

Once again, she was reminded to listen to her good sense, instead of letting her emotions get the better of her.

But to her great relief, Frankie just shook his head. "I'm here to talk about tonight."

Jill frowned. "Tonight? What's tonight?" If there was a group outing, her sisters hadn't mentioned it, but then, they'd been too busy speculating about her personal life to mention their weekend plans.

"Dinner at Concetti's," Frankie said with a smile. "My treat."

Jill narrowed her eyes at him. It was hardly his treat considering that he owned the place, or at least, his family did.

"Just you and me?" she asked, her mind racing nearly as quickly as her pulse.

He grinned easily. "You and me. Some wine. Good food."

"And your mother," Jill gave him a hard stare. "She'll see us together, Frankie."

He nodded, chewing his lip. "Yep. Yep, she will."

"Wait a minute." Jill crossed her arms as she began to see what was going on here. "Do you *want* her to see us together? Because I haven't even agreed to go with you to your cousin's wedding yet. And the more I think about this, I'm not sure I can go along with this."

A Wish Come True

"Too late."

The words were so clipped, and spoken so quickly, that Jill had to pause and process what she'd just heard.

She stared at him, waiting for the punchline to his joke, but her mind was starting to spin and she felt more than a little breathless.

Finally, when she was certain that she hadn't misunderstood anything, but rather was starting to understand far too much, she bulged her eyes and snapped, "Too late?"

A few of the patrons glanced up from their pastries, making her face heat.

Taking a big breath, she exhaled and started again. "Too late, Frankie?" she whisper-shouted. She stared into his deep-set eyes imploringly. "Please tell me that you didn't tell Maria that we're dating!"

"I didn't," Frankie said firmly.

Oh, thank goodness. Jill almost started laughing from relief.

But then, after what appeared to be a rather large gulp, he said, "Debbie might have."

Jill's eyes burst open. "Debbie from the flower shop?"

"I guess she heard it from Erika McCoy, who was at the bar, who saw us together, and one thing led to another and…"

And Erika was Debbie's niece. Of course.

"So now they all think that something is going on between the two of us." Jill kicked herself for wearing that dress and keeping her hair down. And the makeup! Of course there'd be talk.

"You could have corrected your mother," Jill told Frankie. "You could have set the rumors straight."

Olivia Miles

"But why do that if you end up coming to Gia's wedding?" Frankie clasped his hands together, pleading. "Just play along, Jill. For two weeks."

"Two weeks?" she all but shrieked, but then lowered her voice, giving him a long look that showed she wasn't amused. "First, it was one night. Now, two weeks?"

"We had a nice time last night, didn't we?" Frankie grinned.

Jill felt her cheeks flush. She had had a nice time. She just hadn't stopped to think that maybe he had too. Now, she looked up at him, feeling flattered.

Which was probably exactly how he wanted her to feel. Frankie might struggle to find a long-term girlfriend, but he was never shy of a date.

And that begged the question, didn't it? Why her?

"Why me?" she asked, giving him a hard look.

He blinked, seeming surprised by the question.

"You always have a girl in your life, even if they don't last very long. So why not ask out some pretty girl at a bar in Mapleton?" She was fully aware that the next town over was better grounds for mingling, or at least Carly liked to tell her, at least once a week.

"You know Mamma," Frankie said. "She doesn't ever like the girls I bring home. But...she likes you."

Again with the flattery. And again, Jill felt herself succumb to it.

Bristling, she said, "Well, the feeling is mutual. And that's precisely why my answer is no."

"No?" Frankie all but cried.

Jill started organizing the pastry case. She could always

87

tell when her sisters were stationed out front because it wasn't quite as orderly as she might have preferred.

"No," she said, shaking her head firmly. She looked up into his eyes, willing herself not to get too soft when she saw the desperation in them. "I don't like the idea of misleading people."

"Oh, I wouldn't say that's what we're doing," Frankie said, following her down the other side of the counter as she shifted baskets. "People saw what they wanted to see last night. We're not lying. We're just minding our own business. Is it our problem if others can't do the same?"

Jill thought about her sisters, especially Carly, and even Nana, who didn't mind crossing the occasional boundary. Their intentions, like Maria Concetti's, were in the right spot, but sometimes their words and actions were a little unappreciated.

"People will talk even more when you break up with me in two weeks," Jill pointed out. "I don't like the idea of being on the receiving end of their pity."

"But if we do it the other way around, Mamma will be in here first thing the next morning."

Jill almost shuddered at the thought of how Maria would treat the girl who had broken her beloved son's heart. So far as she knew, it hadn't happened yet.

"I'd never want to upset your mother," she insisted.

"Then don't," Frankie said. "She wants you to come to dinner. Why not make her happy, for a couple of weeks at least?"

"I should say no," Jill said, shaking her head, and she really, really should. But Frankie raised a few good points, and the bigger, more pressing issue was that maybe it didn't matter what she said or agreed to. Maybe things were already in motion. As Frankie had said, people saw what they wanted to see last night. And trying to deny it might be more trouble than it was worth.

Frankie's mouth lifted into a grin. "But that sounds an awful lot like a yes."

"Only because I don't see a way out of it now," Jill said reluctantly. Not just with Maria, or Debbie, but no doubt news had traveled to Nana by now, too. And if it hadn't, Carly would surely tell her before nightfall.

"So you'll come to dinner tonight?" he asked.

"As a friend," she said, because that's what they were. What they always had been.

Even if that's not what they would be leading anyone else to believe.

chapter seven

Frankie shouldn't have been surprised that his mother insisted on reserving the best table in the restaurant for his so-called date with Jill Parker considering that it was within earshot of where she usually stood when she wasn't back in the kitchen.

The candle was lit, the single rose in the small vase fresh, and Mamma had brought his cousin Tony in to cover his shift.

"So you won't feel pressured to call it an early night," she told Frankie with an exaggerated wink.

Frankie wasn't sure what Mamma's expectations of to-night were, and he was beginning to regret not coming up with an excuse—that Jill had to work or stay home with her dog. Or that they wanted some privacy.

That was probably the only excuse that would have worked, and something told him that Jill wouldn't have gone for it.

"I think I'll go outside and wait for Jill," he replied.

"Wait!" Mamma cried. "You aren't going to pick her up at her house?"

"She only lives around the corner," Frankie told his mother, even though that wasn't the reason why he had been pacing the kitchen for the last fifteen minutes and then watched Mamma lovingly set the table just for him. Jill had made it very clear that she would meet him at the restaurant after she'd tended to her puppy, and he didn't want to push his luck.

"Oh!" Maria held her hands to the sky and shook her head. "I thought I raised you right! First, you only take the girl out for a drink, and now you can't even be bothered to escort her to dinner. Is it any wonder even Enzo found a wife before you? And he doesn't have your good looks."

It was never a good sign when they fell back on the subject of Enzo and Christa, and now Frankie was regretting not at least pretending to escort Jill to dinner.

"Go," Mamma said, giving him a little push. "Get outside, walk toward Jill's house. I can only pray you get there before she's left. Show her what a gentleman you are, Frankie. Your father never would have dreamed of letting me meet him somewhere."

"Those were different times, Ma," Frankie reminded her. He often heard about the many ways his father had swept Maria Rosetti, as she was known back then, off her very feet, sometimes quite literally, when it came to his moves on the dance floor. "Jill…"

He paused. There were many things he could say about Jill Parker. She was serious, often too much for his taste.

And focused. Dedicated. Relentless. He could still remember the time she had come in second place in a class spelling bee, and wrote out the incorrect word ten times in her notebook at lunch when everyone else was just having a bit of fun.

Now, thinking of that look of consternation on her face, he grinned.

"You think this is funny?" Mamma cried. She pushed his shoulders. "Go. Pick that girl up at her house. What will she tell her grandmother? What will people say? Don't embarrass me, Frankie!"

"Jill is an independent woman," Frankie explained.

Now Mamma's eyes flashed. "And I'm not? I've been running this restaurant for twenty years on my own since your father died! Just because Jill is a smart businesswoman doesn't mean she doesn't appreciate a bit of romance."

Frankie thought about that for a moment, knowing that it was probably true, or at least true enough that he couldn't argue with his mother. But Jill had never seriously dated to his knowledge, not that he kept tabs on such things.

But now, as he stepped outside, and saw Jill coming around the corner, he wondered if his mother had a point. For a moment, he wasn't even sure it was Jill. In a black dress that flared at the waist and hit her knee, his gaze dropped to her legs that teetered slightly in heels. Her blond hair was down again today, bouncing slightly at her shoulders, and as she approached he saw that the lipstick she wore brought out the pink in her cheeks. And her eyes—had they always been so blue?

"You look beautiful," he said when he'd caught up to

her, without thinking, because it was true. She did. Gone were the frown lines and the pinched lips. She seemed lighter. Happier, even.

For a moment, it was easy to forget that this was all a ruse until she pursed her lips and said, "You don't need to flatter me. Your mother can't hear us from here."

Frankie glanced over his shoulder to where his mother was stepping outside with a bottle of wine for a couple at a table on the sidewalk only a few yards behind where he stood.

"You so sure about that?" he said. Then, hearing Mamma clearing her throat loudly behind him, he extended his arm to Jill. "Shall we?"

Her cheeks flushed brighter but she slid her hand through the crook of his arm as he led her into the restaurant and over to the table in the corner. Knowing that his mother would be watching, discreetly or not, he pulled out Jill's chair and then helped her to scoot it back under the table.

If he didn't know Jill better, he'd say she looked pleased when he dropped onto the seat across from her.

Casting a glance over her shoulder, he locked eyes with his mother, who was rapidly approaching the table. Frankie stifled a groan, wishing he could warn Jill but knowing that there wouldn't be any time.

Mamma was on a mission. And tonight, Jill was it.

"Ah, Jill!" Mamma leaned down to hug Jill. "I can't tell you how happy it makes me to see you here tonight! And so beautiful!"

Mamma stopped gushing only to toss a less-than-subtle glance at Frankie.

Jill's cheeks seemed to flame. "Oh, it's just an old dress."

"Old can be beautiful and beautiful is what it is. Just like you. Inside and out. When my Frankie told me that he was inviting one of the Sunrise Sisters to dinner I knew that my son had finally come to his good senses!"

Jill laughed nervously, but it was clear that she was enjoying herself.

Frankie, however, not so much.

"This hair! You should wear it down more often!" Mamma continued.

"I always wear it back when I'm working at the bakery," Jill explained. "I only wear it down for special occasions."

Now Mamma looked as if she might burst with joy. "And this is a special occasion indeed! My son and Jill Parker! I could take a picture to make this moment last longer in my heart!"

"Mamma—" Frankie gave her a stern look and to Jill, an apologetic one. He reached for his water glass, hoping it would cool him down. He was starting to sweat, and it had nothing to do with the heat from the nearby kitchen.

"Oh, but don't you want to capture this moment?" Mamma pressed. "A photograph of your first dinner at Concetti's together. It will be one to show the children someday when they take over the place."

Frankie choked on his water and set the glass back on the table.

"Oh, fine, fine." Mamma gave Jill a conspiratorial wink and then whispered, "Maybe later on."

"Mamma—" Now Frankie's tone gave no room for argument.

"Now, I won't interrupt your romantic evening," Mamma continued as if she hadn't heard him. She plucked a bottle of wine from the nearby rack and presented it to them with a flourish, as she usually only did when the mayor and his wife came to dine. "But here's a bottle of our best wine. And I'll bring you both out some bruschetta to start. Light on the garlic." She waggled her eyebrows at Jill, whose brow pinched in confusion for a moment before the implication registered.

Frankie sank his face into his hand and closed his eyes. He wouldn't be surprised if Jill had gotten up and left by the time he opened them, but to his relief, only Mamma was gone.

Jill looked more shell-shocked than she'd been the night he'd delivered her food earlier this week.

"She's not expecting us to kiss, is she? Here?" Jill all but hissed across the table

Frankie poured two glasses of wine with a heavy hand.

"I wouldn't put it past her," he said. Then, seeing the horror on Jill's face, he grinned. "Don't worry. I'm told I'm a very good kisser."

She rolled her eyes and took her glass. "Ah, yes. I've heard a few stories."

Now Frankie felt his smile slip. He knew this town was full of talk, but he also thought Jill stayed out of all that.

"You mean...at the bakery?" His mouth felt dry. He dated his fair share, but few of the women were from Hope Hollow. He'd made sure to be careful with the local pool, knowing that things could be messy if they didn't work out.

Which they never did.

A Wish Come True

Now, he saw the corners of her mouth twitch and he realized she was getting back at him.

"A sense of humor, I see." He hadn't realized that she had it in her. "Funny, the Jill Parker I knew didn't have one of those back in school."

She shook her head at him. "That was decades ago, Frankie. Besides, good grades were important to me."

"Nothing wrong with that," he said. "Actually, I always admired you."

She looked at him sharply, as if waiting for him to follow that up with a joke, only he was being completely serious.

"I mean it," he said. "You had a way of staying focused. That was something I struggled with in school, especially after…"

Her eyes filled with sympathy. "After you lost your father? I understand."

And maybe she did, considering that she'd lost her mother around the same time he'd lost his father. Only unlike Jill, whose father had skipped town shortly after Carly was born, he still had his mother, while she only had her grandmother.

"It must have been hard being the only child," she said, reminding him of something else she'd had—sisters.

"Mamma has a big family," he said. He didn't want to push things by mentioning that she'd be meeting them all at the wedding in two weeks. The last thing he needed was for Jill to change her mind with Mamma watching.

Sure enough, from the corner of his eye, he saw Mamma poke her head around the door and seem to wait

96

for the right moment to carry over their appetizer. He managed to smile.

"Mamma needs me," he said, knowing it was true. "And I don't mind that one bit."

"Nor should you," Jill agreed. "But it's funny, I used to think that my grandmother needed me. To shoulder responsibility with my sisters, to step in as their parent figure, and later take over the bakery. Lately, though, I've come to realize that all she wants is for me to be happy."

Maria took that moment to walk over to the table and set down the plate. "Ah, good, and the wine is poured. Why don't I turn the music down a little so you two can talk more freely?"

Frankie slid his eyes to his mother. More like so she could eavesdrop more easily.

"It's all fine, Ma," he assured her.

Jill smiled up at Mamma. "This looks delicious. I can't remember the last time I was treated to such a nice meal after work."

Mamma gave Frankie a pointed look and walked away.

"Bruschetta without the garlic." Frankie shook his head. "Mamma must have picked it out piece by piece."

"I'll still eat it." Jill chuckled. "I hate to disappoint her."

"Careful what you wish for," Frankie warned, but catching Jill's eye across the table he realized that kissing her wouldn't be so strange at all. She wasn't the gangly, intense girl he always thought of when he pictured her.

Maybe she never was.

"Oh, everything at Concetti's is delicious," she said, brushing off his concern.

"Thank you," he said and sincerely meant it. His family prided themselves on sharing good food with good people, and they didn't take compliments lightly.

"Especially your pizza sauce," Jill replied pertly.

And just like that, Frankie was reminded that this was not a date at all, but rather, an agreement.

"So they all say," he replied, helping himself to another sip of wine.

"So why be so reluctant to share it?" she asked.

He stared at her for a moment, this girl he'd known all his life, and yet suddenly felt like he didn't know very well at all. With her hair falling loosely at her shoulders, she looked softer and more open, but her eyes bore the same intensity and focus. And tonight, it was on him.

He swallowed another sip of wine against the strange feeling of being on the receiving end of her attention, and not in an idle, casual way like he was used to in the past.

"Oh, I'm sure you have plenty of family recipes that you don't openly share," he said.

Jill nodded as if the answer was acceptable enough, and he was relieved that the subject could be dropped. He still felt a little sick when he thought of what he'd agreed to, but then he reminded himself what he was getting out of this deal. He'd promised his father to not just carry on that recipe, but something more, too. Something bigger.

To make Mamma happy. And Mamma deserved to go to a family wedding and enjoy herself.

Just like he deserved to attend the function without having to mingle with random women while his aunts looked on and then gave their commentary.

"Can I ask you a question?" Jill leaned across the table. In the candlelight, her eyes seemed to glow as a small smile curved her mouth.

"Anything," Frankie said, feeling his heart speed up.

"Is your mother going to stare at our table all night long, or just for the first course?"

Frankie burst out laughing, a sound loud enough to catch the attention of the diners at the other end of the room. Normally, Mamma might flash him a scolding look for disrupting the mood, but tonight she caught his eye and beamed.

"Probably all night," he told Jill, still laughing. "And it's not like we can skip out on the dessert course."

"Of course not!" Jill said. "Dessert's the best part of a meal."

"You would think that, being a baker," he teased.

"My grandmother probably wouldn't forgive me if I didn't." She pushed her fork around the plate. "It's funny, isn't it? Here we are, both in our thirties, and the older generations still hold so much power over us."

"Only because we let them," Frankie countered. "Which I do."

"Because you can't imagine letting your mother down?" Jill asked.

Frankie nodded. "That and because I know all my mother wants is what's best for me."

Jill smiled. "That's true. Which begs the question why you wouldn't want to let her fix you up?"

"Because when I find the right woman, I'll know." Frankie shrugged. "I'm not in a rush."

Jill sighed. "My grandmother was thrilled to hear I got a dog because she said now I'll be forced to leave the house more. Funny, because some people would see a dog as a reason to stay in more."

"You like staying in," Frankie observed.

He waited to see if Jill would take offense but she just nodded. "I do. I'm tired after a long day at the bakery, and I socialize a lot with the customers throughout the day, too. By the time I'm off work, I like to relax and enjoy the quiet for a bit. But…"

Frankie sensed her hesitation. "But it doesn't leave much opportunity to meet anyone?"

"None," Jill confessed.

"And do you want to meet someone?" Frankie asked out of curiosity.

Jill paused then said, "It would be nice to find what my sisters have. But even their roads have been rocky."

"Love isn't for the faint of heart," Frankie agreed. "But I'd like to think it's worth it."

Jill nodded, seeming pensive.

Frankie held up his wineglass. "I think we need a toast, then. To fake dates…until true love finds us."

"Shh," Jill said, glancing nervously over her shoulder.

"Don't worry, Mamma is tending to the sidewalk tables," Frankie said, though he wouldn't be surprised if she had a listening device tucked into that flower arrangement, come to think of it. "To fake dates," he said again, this time in a whisper.

"And well-intentioned relatives," she added, lifting hers.

"We might be able to get away with no kiss at the end of the night," Frankie said. "If you let me walk you home."

"It's only right around the corner," Jill started to protest, but then, giving him a little smile she set down her wineglass and said, "But…that would be nice."

Yes, Frankie thought as he watched Mamma pass their table with a satisfied smile. It would.

*

"Thank you," Jill said, once they were stopped in front of her house. The porch light was on even though it wasn't completely dark outside yet. "The food was delicious."

"It's me who should be thanking you," Frankie said. "First bruschetta with no garlic, and then having to explain to Mamma why our dinner only took an hour and six minutes."

Jill laughed. "I do have a dog to think about now. Do you think she expected us to stay until closing time?"

"I just know that I'll probably have to circle the block a few times before I head back." Frankie joked, but Jill knew there was truth in his words, too.

She hesitated, knowing that she needed to get inside to Toffee but also realizing that she didn't exactly mind Frankie's company. And she did hate the thought of upsetting Maria Concetti, especially when she'd been so excited to have Jill at the restaurant tonight.

Guilt pulled at her chest when she thought of how disappointed the poor woman would be in two weeks when she found out that there was no chance of Jill becoming a future daughter-in-law. It was almost enough to make Jill consider hanging around a little longer.

Or regret ever going along with this plan.

But then she remembered that she hadn't exactly agreed to it—more like she'd fallen into it.

"You could come in for a bit," Jill offered. Then, seeing the way Frankie's brows pulled together, she felt her cheeks heat. "I mean…if you don't want to raise suspicion."

"I'd like that," Frankie said, taking the last step onto the porch. "If I'm not putting you out."

"Not unless you mind playing fetch with my little fur-ball," Jill said as she fumbled for the key in her bag. The sound of the lock being turned set off Toffee's barking, and by the time she hurried to the back of the house to release him from the laundry room, he burst right past her at full speed and straight toward Frankie, who stood in the hallway, as if still not completely sure he'd been invited in.

"I can make coffee," she said, if only to have something to do. Meeting Frankie in public was one thing, but being alone, here in the house, was new territory.

"I can take little Toffee around the block if you'd like," Frankie was already pulling his lead from the hook near the front door.

"Oh!" Jill never failed to recognize how helpful Frankie was. "Thank you!"

She smiled as she kicked off her shoes and disappeared into the kitchen to begin preparing the coffee. The radio on the counter usually kept her company in the early mornings before the sun rose and she was getting ready for the day, but this time she turned the dial to a music station, letting its sound softly fill the room.

By the time Frankie returned with Toffee, both were

grinning from ear to ear and the smell of coffee was filling the house.

"He gave me a workout!" Frankie exclaimed as Jill bent to remove Toffee's collar.

"He tugs a lot. I need to work on training him. We usually close the bakery early on Sundays, so hopefully, I can make some progress with him tomorrow." She motioned to the counter. "Cream? Sugar?"

"I'm guessing I don't come into the bakery enough if you don't know my order by now," Frankie admitted.

"Oh, I think I can remember." Jill thought about the last time Frankie had stopped in for his usual breakfast, which was probably a few weeks back. "Cream. No sugar. And you like our chocolate croissants."

"I don't know whether to be flattered or scared," Frankie replied with a pleased grin.

He came to stand beside her at the small counter where she was preparing two mugs. It was a tight space, and one that Jill didn't use very much, but with his large frame, it felt even smaller. She felt the heat of his body when his arm brushed hers, and the musky scent of his skin, unfamiliar in the house.

But not entirely unwelcome.

A squeaking sound started in the living room and slowly grew louder.

Jill laughed. "I think Toffee's trying to tell us something. Should we go sit?"

She led Frankie into the living room and looked between the sofa and the armchair, deciding where to sit.

Finally, because the toy bin was closest to the sofa, she

took her usual spot. Frankie didn't stop to analyze the seating arrangement. He just sat beside her.

"Is this your first pet?" he asked, rolling a ball to Toffee, who happily chased it.

Jill nodded. "Growing up it was a full house, and we were always busy at the bakery. But I'm sure you've heard that my grandmother has a puppy too now."

"I've seen her walking Sugar around town." Frankie shook his head in wonder. "Sharon Parker. Married. With a puppy."

"I know," said Jill, setting her coffee mug down on a coaster. "It certainly puts pressure on me. I'm running out of excuses for staying single."

"Staying single and being single are very different things," Frankie pointed out. He plucked another toy from the bin and tossed it to Toffee.

"Spoken from someone who is rarely unattached," Jill said. "So tell me, why haven't you found the right one yet?"

Frankie leaned back against the couch. "Well, that's a double-sided question. There were a few girls that didn't pass Mamma's muster."

Yes, Jill was more than familiar with the stories that ranged from funny to silly to a little picky, but then, that was Maria for you. She was a woman of strong opinions, and she wasn't shy about sharing them.

"Is that the deciding factor then?" Jill asked. "Your mother?"

Frankie hesitated and then deferred answering by raking a hand through his hair, causing it to stand a little on end.

Jill resisted the urge to pat it back into place, but she couldn't fight her smile when she sipped her coffee.

"What?" Frankie asked, sitting up straighter. "Do I have something on my face?" He wiped at his cheeks.

"You don't have anything on your face," Jill assured him. She hesitated and then reached out to brush at his hair, pulling her hand back when her eyes met his. "There. Sorry," she added.

"Typical Jill," Frankie said, shaking his head, even though he was smiling. "You like everything in its place."

"Is that so bad?" she remarked.

When he looked at her, all hint of amusement was gone. "Not at all."

Jill felt her heart begin to pound and she blinked quickly, then reached for the closest dog toy she could find and hurled it across the room, sending Toffee off to chase it.

"Well, I should probably get back to the restaurant or I'll be in trouble with Mamma for other reasons." Frankie gave Jill a no-nonsense look. "She's a very traditional woman."

"Oh, I know. It's one of the things I admire about her." Toffee came running back to Jill, without the toy, and she scooped him up and stood.

"Good luck training this little guy tomorrow," Frankie said when they'd reached the entranceway, giving the puppy a scratch behind the ears. He put his hand on the doorknob and then paused to look back at Jill. "Maybe I'll see you at the park…or something."

Jill looked at him, wondering if he was eluding to another fake date, but his eyes were sincere, questioning even.

"Yeah," she said. "Maybe."

"I mean, I wouldn't want to miss an opportunity to see Toffee," he said.

Jill fought off a smile, forcing her most serious face as she nodded. "Of course. He's irresistible."

She watched Frankie step out onto the porch and then slowly closed the door behind him, thinking that it might be nice to run into him tomorrow…even if it was just because she wouldn't deprive Toffee of some extra attention.

And even if it might give people something to talk about.

chapter eight

If word had gotten out about Jill's dinner at Concetti's last night, her sisters managed to not let on, and by the time the Sunday morning rush had dwindled, Jill was starting to relax into her day. The cinnamon rolls were always a big seller on weekends, dating back to when she was just a child, and the trays were now empty. Any customers that came in before they closed would be looking for coffee or a box of muffins or assorted pastries to take home for a relaxing brunch.

The bell jingled, signaling another customer, and Jill heard Becca say, "I hope that they're not looking for a cinnamon roll. I hate disappointing people."

"It's their fault for sleeping in," Carly said, pushing through the kitchen door.

But when Jill turned to shake her head at her sister, she saw Carly's expression transform. Following her gaze, Jill saw the cause for excitement. Debbie from the flower shop had just come in, and while her visits were not an infrequent occurrence (the woman certainly had a sweet tooth), the beautiful bouquet of pink flowers she held in both hands certainly was.

"I bet they're from Jonah," Carly said to Becca, whose smile was equally hopeful.

"Oh, I'm sure they're from Nick," Becca said in return. "Jonah knows I wouldn't want him spending anything on me when he's trying to build his new restaurant."

Still, she watched as Debbie approached and set the vase on the counter. The three sisters admired the assorted blooms as if each daring the other to ask who was the recipient.

"Well," Debbie finally said to them. "Aren't you going to read the card?"

Jill and Becca motioned to Carly. It was likely from Nick, after all. The pair had been dating for months, and surely some anniversary or special occasion had come around by now.

But when Carly licked her lower lip and plucked the card from its plastic holder, her smile slipped for one telling second until turning coy.

"They're not for me."

"Oh!" Becca's cheeks flushed a bright pink. "I can't believe Jonah did this—"

"Hate to break it to you, sis, but he didn't." Carly set a gentle hand on Becca's arm before both sisters turned their attention to Jill. "They're for you, Jill."

"Me?" Jill felt herself go pale, all too aware that both of her sisters were staring at her—and Debbie, too.

She swallowed hard and took the card from Carly, not exactly wanting to open it in front of an audience. What could it possibly say? Was this all part of Frankie's ruse? If so, he might have warned her, if only so she didn't have to deal with that gleam in both of her sisters' eyes.

And Debbie's, she thought, glancing at the woman who showed no intention of moving from the other side of the counter, even though Jill very much doubted that she was waiting to place an order for a scone or muffin.

"I can't imagine who would send me flowers," she muttered, only she could imagine, and it could only be one person. And not for the reasons that any of these women believed. "I'll read it later," she said, starting to slip it into her apron pocket.

"And leave us all hanging?" Carly protested. "You just received a beautiful arrangement of flowers. The least you can do is read the card to us!"

Not only had Jill just received a beautiful arrangement, but it was also the first time in her life that she'd ever received flowers. She used to think it was frivolous, but now, she realized what all the hype was about.

Each stem seemed more beautiful than the next, and Debbie had personally tucked each one into the vase until the creation was complete. Yes, it was a bunch of flowers, but it wasn't the same as the mixed bouquets she sometimes treated herself to at the grocery store at the start of each season. These were…personal. These were more than just flowers. They were a gesture.

And one that she also wasn't used to receiving.

She felt her cheeks flush when she reluctantly pulled the

card from her pocket and popped the seal. Carly and Becca leaned over her shoulder, and Debbie scooted the vase to the side to have a better look, even though she must have memorized it word for word by now.

But the moment Jill saw the two brief sentences, she knew that there was no denying anything to her sisters.

"Last night was wonderful. Next time will be even better." Jill didn't need to say who the card was from. It was spelled out, and Debbie had taken the order.

"Last night?" Carly said, eyes wide and darting. "What was last night?"

Jill fumbled to put the card back in its envelope. "Nothing. Just…"

"A romantic dinner at Concetti's!" Debbie interjected. Then, catching three long stares, she waved her hand through the air and said, "Or so I heard."

"It was just dinner," Jill said firmly. Then, to underscore her point, she said to Debbie, "Can I get you a scone or a muffin for your trouble, Debbie?"

"Oh, deliveries are never any trouble!" Debbie insisted. "There's nothing like watching a person's expression unfold when they realize that someone special was thinking about them."

Someone special. Jill couldn't recall ever having "someone special" in her life—until Toffee, that was. And if Frankie was trying to pose as that then he needn't have bothered. Hadn't dinner last night sufficed? Besides, there was no one around to witness today's show—well, other than her sisters.

And that wasn't part of the deal.

"Speaking of someone special, did you hear about the community cookbook we're putting together for our grandmother's birthday?" Jill asked Debbie. She tapped the sign they'd laminated and placed it on the counter. So far they'd already received over a dozen recipes in just a few short days, but they still had a long way to go if they wanted to compile a full book for Nana—and the community. "But please be discreet. We want it to be a surprise."

Debbie looked momentarily rattled at the topic shift, but she leaned in closer to read the details. "What a wonderful idea! Of course, nothing that I could contribute would be anywhere near as delicious as something Sharon could come up with herself."

"Oh, I doubt that," Becca assured Debbie. "What makes it special is that it comes from you, and you've always been a friend to Nana. There's nothing she cherishes more than food that's made with love."

"And no place in town knows that better than this bakery," Debbie remarked. Then, after a suggestive glance in Jill's direction. "Or Concetti's, of course."

Oh boy. Jill was about to say that she couldn't agree more, which was why she'd be including the sauce recipe, but she knew that it wasn't a done deal, yet, and besides, Debbie might say something to Maria, and she wasn't entirely sure how that would go over.

No, it was better to keep some things to herself.

Or rather, all things, when it came to her little agreement with Frankie.

"On that note, I have another someone special to get home to soon," Jill said, picking up her arrangement, which was surprisingly heavy. "I'll go put these in the kitchen until we close up in half an hour."

"Oh, but you haven't told us about last night!" Carly said.

"Or what's planned for next time," Debbie added, so eagerly that Jill almost laughed. There was no doubt that Debbie had every intention of sharing Jill's answer with Maria.

"I guess it's my little secret," Jill said with a shrug as she slipped through the kitchen door.

Along with the bigger one she was now keeping.

*

Jill spent over an hour at the park in an attempt to burn off some of Toffee's energy and finally decided that she'd only ended up spending most of her own. For a dog with such little legs, he could easily outrun her, and she wasn't exactly out of shape.

She didn't make much time for exercise either, though. But that was before she got Toffee. Now, her routine was different, with breaks in the day for walks and fresh air.

For trips to the park that she had only walked past in recent years, nearly forgetting the days that she used to play here as a child with her sisters, her mother usually trailing not far behind, walking these very paths she now took with Toffee.

She felt the familiar tug in her chest every time she thought of the woman she'd lost as a teenager. Being in the bakery always made her feel closer to her mother, gave her a sense of purpose in the early days after her death, and later, a way to honor their memories.

But being here stirred up other thoughts and feelings—ones that she realized she'd buried somewhere along the way. Or maybe, chose to forget.

Dropping onto a bench, she watched the children playing on the playground from a distance, wondering if she should pull out her phone and text a thank you to Frankie or scold him for drawing her sisters into this when she heard her name being called from the direction of the road.

A strange sense of warmth spread over her when she saw Frankie approaching—not because it saved her from having to reach out on her own, but because he'd shown up, just like he'd said he would.

But then, when wasn't Frankie a man of his word? Never, and maybe that was part of the problem.

Frankie was reliable, and kind, and he'd been a fixture in her life for as far back as she could remember. She'd never had to doubt him or think about him in any other way.

Until now.

"I was just about to text you," she said as he approached.

"Ah, now, you flatter me. I hope you weren't waiting for long."

She gaped at him until she realized that, as usual, he was just trying to get a rise out of her. She shook her head, laughing, and held tighter to the leash as Toffee pulled to greet him.

"I was going to text you to say thank you. And also ask for an apology," she added.

Frankie looked at her in confusion as she rose to her feet.

"You know, about this morning," she said, glancing at him as they let a couple of kids on bikes pass by them. Toffee gave them his best warning bark—high-pitched but so heartfelt that she and Frankie were both momentarily distracted.

"You have a fine watchdog there," Frankie told her.

"Watch out, he likes to chew ankles," she replied. "Especially mine."

He laughed, but then tipped his head. "What happened this morning?"

She looked at him, then, sensing that she would have to spell it out, that she'd have to work for it because he was having a go with her. Finally, huffing out a breath, she said, "The delivery?"

But Frankie's brow furrowed deeper. "What delivery?"

Jill shook her head and stopped walking again. "The flowers! They were beautiful, Frankie. Really. Completely unexpected. You didn't have to, but I will say it resulted in quite a reaction from Debbie. As well as my sisters," she added, less pleased.

Frankie stopped to stare at her. "I have no idea what you're talking about."

She blinked at him. "You sent me flowers."

"I'm sorry, Jill. But I didn't."

She waited for the gleam to reappear in his eyes, for his mouth to crack into a smile, and for that deep rumble of laughter to fill the otherwise quiet spot in nature.

Instead, she realized with a hot flush of horror that he didn't know what she was talking about at all. That he hadn't sent the flowers.

"But if you didn't send them, who did?"

No sooner were the words out of her mouth than the answer came to her. Frankie briefly closed his eyes and then, raking a hand through his hair, muttered a string of Italian words that she couldn't hope to understand and should probably never repeat in front of Maria anyway.

"Mamma must have sent them!" Frankie shook his head.

Jill nodded. Yes, now that she thought about it, it did seem like something Maria would do. And for some reason, even though she knew that it was all for show, and that "someone special" hadn't been thinking of her, she realized by the disappointment that settled in her chest that it was sort of nice thinking that someone had.

"You could have taken the credit, you know," Jill said, trying to lighten the mood. But now Frankie's face was as red as her own, if not from embarrassment then from anger. "Don't be mad at her, Frankie. She was just trying to help."

"Oh, I know. But her definition of help was lost in translation!" Frankie muttered a few more words under his breath and then turned to Jill with an apology in his eyes. "I'm sorry, Jill."

"For what? It wasn't your doing." She sighed. "Although now it's nearly impossible for me to convince my sisters that nothing is going on with us beyond friendship."

"Is that such a bad thing?" he asked.

She had to admit that it was nice having a break from them encouraging her to get away from the bakery more often. "I don't like being dishonest with my family."

"But you said yourself that they're eager to see you in a relationship. Now they're happy. So you can be too."

She laughed lightly and wagged a finger at him. "You have a remarkable way of justifying this."

"I'm sorry," he said, setting a hand on his chest. "You know I didn't want to make this complicated. But it seems that our family members have decided to see what they want to see. And in my case, run with it."

"Well, the whole town probably knows by now." Jill groaned inwardly. "There's no way that my grandmother hasn't heard something."

"I'm sure she was on Mamma's speed dial last night!" Frankie exclaimed, then set a heavy hand on her shoulder as his dark eyes turned pleading. "Think you can forgive me, Jill?"

She looked into his eyes, feeling a pull between them, just long enough to make her come to her senses and glance away, across the park.

"As you said, it wasn't your doing," she replied. Besides, it was difficult to stay mad at Frankie for long. Always had been. Even back in school. Sure, he liked to yank her chain, but he wasn't malicious about it. And sometimes, though she'd never admit it, maybe not even to herself fully, she needed the levity.

Those were some tough years when her mom got sick and then passed away when Jill was fifteen. She coped by focusing on what she could control, but she never made much time for fun. Frankie had a way of giving her a small dose of it, however uninvited his efforts might have been.

"I have a confession to make, actually," Frankie said as they continued their walk.

"Oh?" she asked. "What's that? Not another dinner at Concetti's tonight?" She couldn't help but panic. The meal had been wonderful and watching Frankie be on the receiving end of someone's teasing for a night had certainly been entertaining, but she wasn't sure she could face Maria again, not after the woman had gone so far as to send Jill flowers, however surreptitiously.

"Nah, tonight I'm at the fire station so you're off the hook," Frankie replied.

For some reason that didn't delight her as much as it might just a few days ago. Jill knew that her sisters would be busy with their boyfriends and Nana would be spending a quiet evening with her new husband.

"So what is it that you need to tell me?" If he was going to tell her that he had no intention of sharing the sauce recipe, then she'd really have no choice but to turn around and go home now.

But she knew that Frankie would never do that. He was a man of his word.

Well, except when he was pretending to fake date her.

"This is my second stop at the park today," Frankie said.

She stared at him, trying to process what he was saying, but knowing that there was only one meaning.

"You came here earlier?" she asked.

"I wasn't sure what time you'd be arriving," he said simply. "And I couldn't miss a visit with this little pup." He looked down at Toffee fondly and was greeted with a tail wag in return.

"Of course," Jill said lightly, trying to hide her pleasure. "You can't disappoint Toffee."

Frankie's eyes met hers when he grinned, revealing those two dimples that he'd inherited from his mother. "Never!"

"Well, I'm glad our timing lined up eventually," Jill said, struggling to hide her smile. "And I don't think Toffee would have let me take him home until he'd gotten an ear scratch from you."

"I am very good at ear scratching," Frankie boasted. Then, giving her a suggestive look, he added, "Along with other things."

She gave him a playful swat as they turned toward the small pond near the back of the park. When she was younger, her mother used to take her and her sisters here to feed the ducks. Carly always loved the babies the most, but what Jill always admired was the way they all followed their mother, so loyally.

Much like she and her sisters had done, and still did.

Much, she thought, glancing at Frankie, like the man beside her did too.

"You are good at making sauce, I'll give you that," she said.

"Oh, sure, but I had a good teacher," he said.

She nodded, knowing that Maria was a natural chef, even if she'd never been formally trained.

"We both learned from the best," Jill agreed, thinking of her mother's patient voice, the way she taught Jill how to cream butter with sugar, and how to scoop out the batter to ensure even-sized cookies.

Her eyes burned and she blinked quickly, warding away tears.

"My mother used to bring me to this park," she said, not sure why she'd voiced it, but feeling like she could. That Frankie, having lost a parent, too, could understand. "It's funny because somehow, I forgot about that until I came here today. I haven't been back in years."

"Well, you'll be making a lot more visits here now that you have this little guy," Frankie said, stopping to give Toffee that scratch he'd promised.

"I will," Jill agreed, already looking forward to it. "But not as much as I'd like. I feel bad leaving him home alone when I'm at the bakery, especially while he's just getting used to things."

"Why don't you let me help out a bit?" Frankie suggested.

"Oh, no," Jill started to protest, but Frankie was already picking up the little dog, who gave him a few licks on the cheek.

Jill had to admit that there was something especially sweet about seeing big, burly Frankie snuggling such a small dog, who looked even tinier in his large hands.

"I'm around a lot during the day this week. Evening shifts only at the station, and you know the restaurant is only open for dinner. I can pop over in the mornings and afternoons and give him some exercise."

It was tempting. And Toffee would certainly benefit, meaning she couldn't exactly refuse.

"You're not trying to get out of giving me the recipe for the sauce, are you?" she asked suspiciously.

He looked so surprised as he set down Toffee and straightened his back that she felt momentarily ashamed for asking. "We have a deal. And I intend to keep it."

She nodded. "I do too."

"So after Gia's wedding, you'll get the recipe," Frankie said, locking her eyes for a moment.

Jill wondered if he was thinking what she was. That the wedding was less than two weeks from now. That already she'd gotten used to his company. That she wasn't sure what it would be like to just see him around town again.

"But for now, I wouldn't mind an excuse to get out of the apartment a bit," Frankie said. "And this little guy is great company."

Jill beamed down at her sweet little puppy, who was taking a rest under the shade of a willow tree, his little tongue hanging out as he panted. "He is."

"So, it's a deal?" Frankie asked. "Or…another one?"

"At least let me pay you," Jill offered. Insisted, really.

But Frankie shook his head. "Nope. Then no deal."

"But a deal implies something in return," she pointed out.

Frankie thought about it for a second and then said, "Okay, then, you save me some treats from the bakery. And don't tell my mother, or she'll warn me about putting on pounds and ruining my physique."

He patted his hard, flat stomach, and Jill's eyes lingered there for a moment before she pulled her attention back to his face, only to see his grin.

"I think it would take more than a few scones or muffins to do that," she said. "Besides, you'll be walking off the calories. With Toffee."

"So we have a deal?" he asked.

"Okay, then," Jill agreed. "And thank you."

"No thanks needed," Frankie said with a grin. "That's what friends are for."

Friends, Jill reminded herself.

chapter nine

Frankie had already started prepping for dinner service when his mother came into the kitchen the next morning, looking only partly guilty when she caught his eye.

"I know about the delivery," he told her. When she feigned innocence by fluttering her eyelashes, he said, "The flowers."

"Oh. That." Mamma washed her hands, taking extra time scrubbing them clean.

Frankie gave her a long look and then went back to the lasagna he was layering. There was no use in having this conversation, not when she was determined to pretend she hadn't done anything wrong.

"We have a cheese delivery today," Mamma said, looking at the calendar she kept on the wall. "You can handle it?"

Frankie nodded. He always handled the big deliveries, and he already knew to expect one today.

"I wasn't sure if you'd be taking another walk," Mamma said, tying on her apron. When he didn't reply, she said, "I saw you over near the park yesterday when I was heading to the market."

Frankie forced himself not to respond, knowing that replying wouldn't do either of them any good. She must not have seen him with Jill or she would have said something by now, and he wasn't about to give her any more reason to speculate.

For a moment, he almost thought about telling her the truth. But then he thought of that list she'd compiled with her sisters—six names deep and still taped to the board where Mamma kept other important notes to herself, usually restaurant related—so he stayed focused on food prep and told himself that in a few minutes, he'd slip away to walk Toffee.

And hope Mamma didn't have a comment on that.

"You're quiet today," Mamma remarked.

Frankie heaved a sigh and pushed the lasagna pan away. "Well, what can I say? Anything I say, you run with it, Mamma!"

"Ah, so you're mad about the flowers," she said, tossing up her hands.

"Mamma, you didn't need to do that," he replied. More like *shouldn't* have done that, he thought, but he couldn't quite bring himself to say it, not when Jill had looked so happy to have received them.

"Didn't need to?" She hooted. "Someone needed to! You think Jill Parker doesn't deserve flowers?"

"I didn't say that." Jill was sweet, smart, stubborn, and

surprisingly appealing. And he would have liked to have been the man who brought that smile to her lips.

But he wasn't that man. He was just playing the part.

"Besides, I wouldn't have had to send the flowers if you'd had the sense to do it yourself!" Mamma mumbled under her breath and got out her ravioli press, a treasured wedding gift and the only one she ever used here in the restaurant.

"We've talked about this before," Frankie said. "It doesn't help when you get involved in my love life." He gave her a knowing look, long enough for her to purse her lips, making an almost painful effort to refrain from what she really wanted to say.

"Remember the woman I met at the festival last spring?" reminded her.

"Who can forget?" Maria snorted. "She was the one who didn't like cheese on her pizza! What's bread with sauce, I ask you?"

"She was lactose intolerant, Mamma," Frankie said firmly, resulting in a little mew from his mother.

Still, Maria just shook her head. "It had nothing to do with her shunning my pizza, Frankie, and you know it."

"She could tell you didn't approve, Mamma," Frankie said. "You scared her off!"

Now Mamma pointed a finger at him, grinning. "Ah, but you didn't go chasing after her, trying to win her back, did you, Frankie?"

"No," he admitted. Only because he didn't exactly feel a connection, not because his mother was annoyed over her dinner choices.

"But imagine if I'd really liked her," he said.

"But you didn't!" Maria shrugged.

Frankie held back a sigh. "Yes, but what if I had?"

"Then I would have happily made that girl an extra-large circle of bread topped with our delicious sauce and delivered it with a smile," Mamma replied, giving him a pat on the cheek.

Frankie shook his head. "You know what the problem is, Mamma? I can never stay mad at you."

"Runs in the family," she said, giving him a wink. Watching him grab his keys, she said, "Where are you going?"

He glanced at the clock. He'd planned to take Toffee for a walk this morning to ensure that he'd be back in time to handle the delivery.

"Nowhere in particular," he replied. Then, more pointedly: "Nowhere that you need to know."

But from the sly twist of her mouth, he had a feeling that it wouldn't stop her from finding out.

*

"Was that Frankie I just saw walk by the window with Toffee?" Carly asked as she approached the counter where Jill was plating their last scone for Mrs. Handler, their old art teacher, long since retired.

Jill thanked the woman and then glanced out the window "It was. He offered to take Toffee out a few times this week when he's not working, and I couldn't exactly deprive my little guy of the extra exercise."

Seeing no other customers, she walked around the

counter and over to the door where she caught a glimpse of Frankie and Toffee as they stopped at the corner. Toffee looked especially small from this distance, nowhere near as big as Frankie's shoes, and Jill felt her heart pull with love when she saw his little tail wiggling while they waited. His tongue hung out happily, and he wore a big grin on his small face.

When the light changed, Frankie made Toffee sit, then rewarded him with a treat, before giving him the all-clear to start walking.

"Wow," Becca breathed beside her.

Jill jumped a little. "I didn't see you there."

"I was wondering what could hold your interest so tightly," Becca observed. "Now I see."

"He's so cute," Jill said, sighing with contentment.

"Ah, so you finally admit that you think Frankie is cute, do you?" Carly remarked from her other side.

Jill looked ruefully at her sister. "I was talking about Toffee. Obviously."

Still, Frankie did look sort of cute. Especially with Toffee as his accessory. She watched as two young women stopped him and then crouched to coo over Toffee, but Jill could see from even this distance that they were also fawning over Frankie.

And Frankie, being Frankie, looked like he was enjoying the attention.

"Just like Nana said," Carly remarked. "Walking a cute little dog like Toffee will get you a lot of social interaction."

"What are you really saying?" Jill asked, ready to turn from the window. She walked back toward the counter, Carly close behind.

"Just that I saw the way those women were looking at Frankie," Carly said.

Across the room where Becca was now clearing a table, Jill saw her sister shake her head. If only Carly could be as sensible as their middle sister. But from the suggestive look on her face right now, it was clear there was no hope of that anytime soon.

"Are you asking if I'm jealous?" Jill stepped behind the counter and surveyed the contents of the pastry case.

"Are you?" Carly countered.

"No," Jill said, her defenses rising, but not only because she wanted to shut down this conversation. The truth was that she had felt a little jealous of the way those women were smiling up at Frankie, and mad at herself for somehow contributing to the opportunity.

After all, wasn't Toffee a great excuse to stop and chat with a cute guy?

Not that Frankie was cute. Well, he was cute. Objectively, of course.

Catching Carly's raised eyebrows, Jill sighed. "I mean, maybe a little jealous on account of Toffee. He's my dog and I enjoy hearing the praise people give him."

"Uh-huh." Still, Carly didn't seem convinced. "And here I thought you didn't appreciate all the praise they were probably giving Frankie."

"You know they only stopped to chat with him because of Toffee," Jill replied, which she immediately realized was the wrong answer when she saw Carly's satisfied grin.

"So you *are* jealous!" She tipped her head. "I guess it comes with the territory when you're dating a man as good-looking as Frankie Concetti."

"Since when did you find Frankie to be good-looking?" Jill stared at her sister.

Carly shrugged. "Since always. I mean, those eyelashes? Those dimples? That smile? Not to mention his body."

"Watch it," Jill warned, but she was laughing. "You wouldn't want this to get back to Nick."

"Oh, Nick knows he has nothing to worry about," Carly said with a dismissive wave. "Frankie is handsome. But…he's always just been Frankie, you know?"

Jill did know. More than she could admit right now.

"What are we talking about now?" Becca asked as she made her back to the counter.

"That Jill landed a hottie," Carly replied.

"Carly!" Jill snapped but then shook her head. She did sound uptight, didn't she? But all this talk about Frankie was making her…uncomfortable.

"Don't you think that Frankie is good-looking?" Carly asked Becca.

"Oh, yeah," Becca said without giving it a second thought.

"You too?" Jill couldn't believe what she was hearing. "But you never showed any interest in him before!"

"Because I wasn't interested," Becca explained. "And you know that Jonah was always the only one for me."

True, but still…

"I just never looked at him that way," Becca added.

Jill nodded. Neither had she.

She picked up a rag and began wiping down the counter, even though she'd already cleaned it so much it was practically shining.

"Oh, look, he's being stopped again," Carly announced from where she now stood near the door.

Jill was almost afraid to look out the window, and when she did, she wished she had listened to her gut. "Nana?" she gasped.

Sure enough, there was Nana, her silver hair pulled back in its usual bun, in her favorite bright pink shirt dress, beaming up at Frankie while Toffee and Sugar got tangled up in each other's leashes.

"I wonder what they're talking about," Carly said, reading Jill's mind as Nana let out what was an obvious peal of laughter even from across the street.

"I don't think I want to know," Jill muttered, turning away.

"Well, Nana looks very happy," Carly remarked.

Jill sighed heavily. She was sure that her grandmother was very happy. And that was what troubled her.

As expected, it only took a few minutes before the door jingled again, and in walked Nana. Through the window, Jill saw Frankie now holding two leads, and already he was gaining double the attention of passersby. Double the dogs, Jill figured.

"Hello, Nana!" the sisters said in unison. Carly quickly flipped the sign for the cookbook, then positioned herself in front of it.

It wasn't uncommon for their grandmother to stop by, although now that she was newly remarried it was certainly less frequent.

"I just popped in to grab a pie if you have one that hasn't been cut yet," Nana said. "I'm having some of the ladies from my garden club over tonight."

"And you didn't want to bake the pie yourself?" Carly slid Jill a look, knowing that this often sparked a reaction from her.

And usually, it did, prompting Jill to remind Nana of her arthritis. Jill felt protective of her grandmother and she always had. As the oldest of the sisters, she felt just as responsible for her younger siblings, especially in the wake of their mother's death. But Jill's mother was Nana's daughter, and as much as her own heart was breaking, she saw the pain in her grandmother's eyes.

Hard work was what got Nana through that difficult time. And Jill, too.

"It was either bake a pie or take Sugar for a walk," Nana said unapologetically. "And who can resist that face?"

All four women turned to the window to admire the little white dog, but Frankie used the opportunity to grin broadly and wave.

"Isn't that a sight?" Nana slanted a glance at Jill.

It was unavoidable, Jill knew. Still, her heart sped up with how best to handle this.

"Frankie is certainly a helpful person," she commented.

"And he told me that he's been helping with Toffee!" Nana said.

"In exchange for a sweet treat, yes." Jill made a mental note to set aside a chocolate croissant for him today. Two, if possible. The guy could eat, after all.

"Is that all it is?" Nana asked innocently, but it was clear from the gleam in her blue eyes that she knew the answer.

"I suppose that Maria told you about my dinner at Concetti's on Saturday night." Jill sighed, wondering if this inquisition was better than the matchmaking conversations she had grown used to in recent months.

"She did," Nana said. "Sounds like a very nice evening."

"It was," Jill replied because it was the truth.

Still, she held her breath, hoping that she wouldn't have to elaborate further, but her grandmother seemed satisfied with the response. She collected the boxed pie from Becca and walked back toward the door.

"I'll let you girls get back to work. Remember, if you need an extra set of hands—"

"Nana," Jill warned.

But Nana was already out the door, exchanging words with Frankie as she reclaimed Sugar's lead.

"It's a good thing I thought to turn the sign for the community cookbook," Carly said, now turning it upright again.

"Quick thinking," Jill agreed, grateful that Carly had kept their secret safe. "We want to keep it a surprise until her party."

"Before I forget," Becca said. "Jonah wants to have a soft opening—before the party. A tasting for his new menu. And you're all invited."

"All?" Jill looked at Becca with confusion.

"I mean, Carly and Nick. And you and…" Becca raised an eyebrow.

Jill laughed as she began combining the leftover muffins into one basket. "If this is your way of alluding to me bringing Frankie, we're far from being a couple."

"Yet," Carly added. "You've gone on two dates. What's wrong with a third? He did take your dog for a walk."

Jill didn't mention that according to their deal, he'd be taking Toffee on plenty more.

"And he's Jonah's friend," Becca pointed out, bringing her attention back to Jill and showing that, unlike their youngest sister, she wasn't feeding into these matchmaking games. "I'm sure that Jonah will invite him if you don't. Zach Mason will probably be there, and maybe a few other people from town. He wants to keep it small, though. And he wants honest opinions!"

"Oh boy," Jill muttered, more about the honest opinions than the thought of spending another evening with Frankie. "You know we'll have to tell him we like everything or he'll be crushed."

Becca winced. "I know. But he wants to use this time to gather information. I can't be his only taste tester, and Robert and Nana are far too polite to say anything to discourage him. They're both just so happy that he's moved back to the area, not that I don't share their feelings."

"So have you given any constructive criticism?" Jill asked.

Becca thought about it for a second. "Oh, a little more salt. A little less heat. Does that count?" When Carly laughed, Becca protested, "But everything he has made is so good, I really can't think of any way for him to improve it."

"That's where having the guys there will help," Carly said. "They'll be a little blunter. Especially Frankie."

"The man does know his flavors," Jill agreed. Especially when it came to that pizza sauce.

"So you'll go?" Becca asked.

"Of course, I'll go," Jill said.

"But you haven't even asked when it is yet," Carly joked.

Jill realized that she'd fallen back on old habits. She'd gotten so used to having a free calendar that she never had to stop and think if she was available before. But now she had a puppy waiting for her at home.

And a few more dates with Frankie. At least between now and his cousin's wedding.

"Put her down for two," Carly told Becca. Then to Jill, she said, "If you don't bring Frankie, I'm setting you up with that Sophia's dad's brother. End of story."

The decision was made, then.

It was almost worth letting her sisters believe that she and Frankie were a couple. If only to keep Carly quiet for at least a couple of weeks.

*

After a long day on her feet, Jill wasn't thinking of anything other than a hot bath and relaxing on the couch with Toffee at her side.

She turned the lock of her front door, smiled when Toffee's barking grew louder and more frantic, and dropped her keys in the bowl on the hall table beside the flower arrangement that was certainly a welcome sight—even if it had been sent to her by Mamma Maria.

It was a reminder that she needed. That this arrangement, unlike the flowers, was fake. But that the people in the community, however meddling, cared about her—even if some might not always agree with how they showed it.

In the laundry room, Toffee had once again made a mess of his toys, which seemed to have grown quite a bit in number.

"Where'd this come from?" Jill asked, opening the baby gate to let Toffee run free. She picked up the small stuffed frog and gave it a squeak. Immediately, Toffee barked in excitement. Clearly, this mystery toy was one of his new favorites.

And it wasn't much of a mystery where it came from either.

Along with the stuffed bunny and the pumpkin and the penguin, she noted. And was that a miniature tennis ball?

And here she thought she was the one spoiling the little guy. It would seem that Frankie was guilty of the same.

Jill picked up the new ball and rolled it across the kitchen floor, watching as Toffee scampered after it. He hadn't yet learned to retrieve his toys, so she tossed the pumpkin, which bounced along before Toffee got his paws on it and gave it a good squeak with his tiny teeth. Jill could have played like this all evening, but she also knew that if they kept going like this, Toffee would either have an accident in the house or be too tired for a walk. And she was losing steam for one as it was.

Best to go now, while she was still wearing her shoes, so she could relax for the night with a bowl of cereal for dinner and ice cream for dessert, as had become her routine most nights.

Or maybe not.

Jill spotted a note on the fridge, trying to read it from across the room without any success. She picked up Toffee and, stepping closer, plucked the note free.

"Look inside."

Her heart beat a little faster, almost afraid of what she might see. Another of Frankie's practical jokes? Something that would make her scream like one of those plastic spiders he talked about—or worse?

If it was a rubber snake, she'd call off this entire arrangement. Sauce and all.

With one eye open she slowly pulled open the door, bracing herself for what might be inside. But inside, next to her cartons of berries and stacks of yogurt was a large takeout bag from Concetti's. And another note.

"Thought you might be hungry. And this time, Mamma didn't interfere at all. (Well, maybe just a little.)"

She pulled in a long breath and let it out happily. It wasn't the food, not that she didn't have that to now look forward to. Or the smell that wafted from the bag when she peeked inside to see a three-course meal: a tomato and basil salad, her favorite pasta on the nights she stopped by for takeout, and of course, Maria's famous tiramisu.

It was that someone was thinking of her.

And that was a feeling she could get used to all too easily, even if going forward it wouldn't be with Frankie.

chapter ten

For the second Wednesday in a row, and probably the only two Wednesdays of her adult life, Jill didn't feel the need to run over to the bakery to work on invoices or purchase orders. Maybe there had never been a reason to spend the day off going to work—it was more that she didn't have any reason to stay away.

But today, she took Toffee for a long walk, came home to a sweet, creamy coffee, and then thought about the upcoming wedding—and what it entailed.

She'd have to buy shoes, and a dress, unless she borrowed another one from Carly, and that would require telling Carly that she was attending this wedding, which was bound to come up—if not from her, then through Maria and grapevine.

She treated herself to one of the skincare masks that Carly had included in the bag of makeup, then sat down with her laptop on the kitchen counter to search for something she could order—discreetly—when she heard a fumbling of locks in the hallway. Her back stiffened. Toffee started barking in panic, a noise even shriller and more energetic than his excited bark, and before Jill could stop him front springing into the hallway, she heard the front door swing open and the sound of heavy feet on her hardwood floors.

"Toffee!" Frankie exclaimed from the other side of the wall. "How did you break free from your gate?"

Jill froze in horror. In her sweatpants and a faded tank top, she hadn't even showered yet. She couldn't imagine what her hair looked like after she'd carelessly tied it up into a messy bun before her walk.

And since when did she care? Frankie had seen her thousands of times in her life, but all this one-on-one stuff made her feel like she was in the spotlight, when she'd always been much more comfortable in the shadows.

"Frankie?" she called from the kitchen, still trying to think of an exit plan. She eyed the back door, thinking of how easy it would be to dash into the backyard, but her plan stopped there. She had no choice, did she? Frankie had let himself into her house. And now she had to face him. Messy hair and frumpy outfit and all.

"Jill?" He sounded surprised that she was home, but as he appeared in the open doorway, holding Toffee, his expression transformed to one of pure glee.

"That happy to see me?" she remarked, still feeling self-conscious about her attire. She wasn't even wearing one of her nice tank tops, but rather, the one she'd slept in. And she knew that the sweatpants were saggy in the rear and did nothing for her hips—but they were practical and comfortable—but not that bad. Not enough for Frankie's eyes to take on that sheen and his grin to turn positively wicked.

"Surprised to see you," he finally said.

"It's Wednesday," she told him. "The bakery is closed on Wednesday."

"Oh." Frankie grimaced. "So technically I just broke into your house."

"I won't call the cops," she bantered. Then, seeing an opportunity, she added, "But if you don't end up giving me the sauce recipe after this, I may have to report you after all."

"A promise is a promise," Frankie said, but his smile had slipped a little. It always did when that sauce was mentioned.

Jill wondered why, but she also didn't want to push things, not when they had an agreement that she was counting on seeing through to the end.

Even if that meant going to the wedding as his date, for all of his mother's extended family to see.

"While I have you, I was wondering how formal this wedding will be," she said. "Is it outdoors, indoors? Venue?"

Frankie was still staring at her strangely. After a long pause, he said, "I honestly don't now. It's a tense subject, so I didn't dare ask for details."

So much for that. Jill knew she could ask Maria, but she wasn't sure she was ready for the conversation that would come from it—and further misleading the woman was not high on her to-do list.

"So is this what you do on your days off then?" Frankie asked, fighting off a smile.

Jill frowned at him. "You mean, hang around my house and get caught up on chores and errands?"

"And..." He gestured to his face, his mouth spreading into a wide grin as her eyes widened in realization.

She set a hand to her cheek, only to find that it felt hard and crusty. The mask was meant to be washed off after five minutes, and she couldn't even begin to calculate how much time had passed since she'd applied it.

"Oh. This. Yes. It's meant to...moisturize," she said, recalling the description on the packaging.

Frankie's brows shot up. "Really? Because it looks like it's starting to...crack."

"Oh?" Jill casually asked, then tried to take a discreet glance at the toaster, hoping to catch her reflection in the metal. Her heart sped up when she saw the green mask now hardened like a shell, cracking in lines near her mouth and corners of her eyes—basically everywhere her face had moved.

And the color. Green really didn't suit anyone, did it?

"I clearly walked in on something," Frankie said, trying not to laugh.

"Well, that's what you get for breaking into someone's house," she replied. The only small blessing was that the mask was covering the dark flush of humiliation in her cheeks.

"So this is what Jill Parker looks like on her days off, when she's home alone, and doesn't expect to see anyone." Frankie's eyes gleamed.

"And what does it look like?" Jill was fully aware of his opinions about her. They were shared by Carly. Likely, others.

"Unexpected," he replied. Then, "In a good way."

"Oh." She couldn't help but be flattered. If not a little confused. She was wearing glorified pajamas, with messy hair, and had a face mask crumbling around the corners of her mouth, one that made the whites of her eyes look a little yellow, too.

Maybe he was teasing her.

But his smile had faded, and instead, the look in his eyes had turned thoughtful.

She cleared her throat. "Well, I should probably get this washed off."

"I guess you won't be needing me to walk Toffee today," Frankie said, stepping back into the hall. "Just as well. We're expecting a delivery at the restaurant soon and I usually handle those."

"Too heavy for Maria?" Jill asked casually, eager to get off the topic of her appearance.

Frankie set down the dog. "It's the supplier. A nice guy. But Mamma avoids him for some reason. There's a story there, probably having to do with an argument over cheese at some point in the distant past."

Jill thought about how Maria Concetti had treated Jonah for weeks after he'd moved back to town—two years after leaving it and breaking Becca's heart.

She could be a grudge holder, but she was also very protective of those she loved.

Jill's stomach swooped at the thought of her upcoming

fake breakup with Frankie but she tried to cover it with a smile, finding it more difficult than even a moment ago to stretch her face.

It must have been obvious because she saw Frankie fight off a smile.

"Well, thank you for coming over," she said, even though she really, really wished that he hadn't.

Frankie paused near the door. "Jonah's having a thing...this Friday. I figured that Becca would have told you. So we're both invited."

Jill nodded. "The question is, how do we act? My sisters think we're dating, thanks to that flower delivery."

"I won't ham it up too much," Frankie promised.

Jill raised an eyebrow, not sure that Frankie was capable of that, given the opportunity, especially when she saw the shine in his dark eyes.

"You're thinking it would be fun to mess with them, aren't you?" she accused.

Frankie's grin turned bashful. "It would be easy..."

"No." Jill shook her head. "I can't lie to my sisters. It's hard enough not telling them the truth."

"You could tell them the truth," Frankie offered. "The only person I'm trying to convince is my mother."

Jill hesitated. As annoying as it was to listen to her sisters' comments about Frankie, it was better than having Carly push her to get out more.

"It's only for another week and a half," she said. "My sisters will have plenty to say when I tell them it's over. I may as well put it off until then."

"So they approve of us dating then?" Frankie looked genuinely curious.

A Wish Come True

Jill grew flustered. If he was fishing for a compliment, she wasn't about to deliver, even if her sisters had both commented on his good looks.

She studied his face now, which had grown even more familiar in recent days, but also, somehow, different. Now, instead of just seeing the dark eyes and dimples, every time she looked at him she saw those eyelashes and that full mouth, darn it.

"I mean…they were surprised. But not…unhappy about it."

"Huh." Frankie jutted his lower lip as he absorbed this information, but it was clear that he had thoughts about it.

"Don't flatter yourself," Jill told him, but she couldn't help but smile, or try to at least. For all of his swagger, she knew that Frankie wasn't vain. And if finding dates came as easily to him as he claimed, he never would have had to ask her to pose as his.

"Nick will be there," Frankie said. "And Jonah. I suppose your sisters have told them that we're dating?"

"Probably," Jill replied. "Have you seen Nick at the station? Has he said anything?"

"Our shifts haven't crossed over since that first night you stopped by," Frankie replied.

"So Friday will be a big night." Jill felt a wave of nerves pass over her stomach, and she wasn't sure if it was from the thought of misleading her loved ones or presenting herself at Frankie's side…in public.

"Consider it a dress rehearsal for the wedding," Frankie said.

And then, Jill really did start to feel sick. It was one thing

142

to spend time with Frankie, have a few laughs, and even have some pleasant conversations. But being around their friends and family took things to a different level.

It made this fake relationship feel a little too real for her comfort.

*

Jonah's new restaurant was on a busy corner in the neighboring town of Mapleton—the same storefront where his parents had once owned and operated a bistro. Jill hadn't crossed the river into this town in a while, but she remembered the greasy diner that had once occupied the spot. Now, she took in the lead-paned windows, space reserved for sidewalk seating, and the sign above the awning that hung over the front door, angled on the corner for all to see.

"The Legacy Bistro," Jill said aloud, squeezing Becca's arm. "It couldn't be more perfect."

"Wait until you see the inside!" Becca's eyes were lit up but it was clear from her energy that she was nervous about tonight and wanted it to be a success for Jonah. His dream of owning his own restaurant was finally coming true, and their plans for a life together were quickly falling back into place.

"Just so you know, I helped pick the light fixtures, so be sure to compliment those," Becca whispered.

"I plan to compliment everything," Jill assured her. "Especially the chef."

Inside, she was relieved to see that they were the first to arrive. The last hour of daylight was filtering through the large windows, but already, Jonah had created an inviting mood. The floorboards were dark and wide. The booths near the windows were cozy, and the bar was shiny and warm. Brass lighting contrasted with the otherwise dark materials, and the white tablecloths gave an elevated touch. This wasn't going to be a hamburger joint.

"I think I just heard my stomach rumble," Jill said, pressing a hand to it, realizing that it might have been nerves. But unlike Becca, she wasn't worried about how the food or ambiance would be received. She was worried about interacting with Frankie in front of their friends and her family.

"I know," Becca said. "Baking is one thing, but neither of us is known for cooking ourselves nice dinners. I haven't eaten this well in years."

"I've been eating surprisingly well this week," Jill admitted. Then, seeing Becca's questioning look she said, "Concetti's. Takeout." More like personally delivered meals left in her fridge by her so-called dog walker. Last night there had been another bag waiting for her, this one containing minestrone, a hearty slice of lasagna, and cannoli.

"And here I thought you were going to tell me that you had another date with Frankie."

Jill knew that she could tell Becca anything. She wasn't just her sister but her best friend, and while she knew that Carly had her best interest at heart, she had a different way of showing it than Becca did.

"About that," she started to explain the situation, but Becca just set a hand on her shoulder.

"You don't need to worry about me teasing you," Becca said. "You get enough of that from our sister. I'm just happy for you, Jill. There's been something different about you lately. Something lighter."

"I do feel a little less stressed," Jill admitted. "All the walks with Toffee are good for me. Fresh air. Exercise."

She waited to see if Becca would comment on her other recent activities, but Becca wasn't one to push, at least, not overtly.

"It's nice to have something to look forward to outside of work," Becca agreed. "You can love what you do, but once you let other things in…you realize what you've been missing."

Jill turned as the door opened and Frankie walked inside.

"Maybe what you've been missing was right here all along," Becca whispered to her before walking back to the kitchen to help Jonah.

Jill took a breath and smoothed the skirt of the simple sundress that had been in Carly's bag of clothes. Like the other nights, she kept her hair down, and like the other nights, Frankie had made an effort with a button-down shirt to replace his usual tee shirt.

But tonight wasn't about putting on an act for Maria's sake. Tonight was about Jonah and Becca. Whatever her sisters gleaned from Jill's interaction with Frankie didn't matter.

Only when Carly and Nick appeared in the doorway before Jill could even approach Frankie, it was clear that it did matter—at least to Jill's family.

"There you two are!" Carly said, giving Frankie a suggestive glance and Jill a quick hug, even though they'd only left each other at the bakery a couple of hours ago. "Wow! Look at this place!"

Jill was happy for the distraction. The restaurant was impressive. And it was the purpose of them all being here. Nick was far too polite to tease Frankie about their newfound closeness, but she saw a few glances pass between them as they walked around the room, marveling over the details.

There was no doubt that the next time they were at the fire station, words would be shared. Jill was just happy she wouldn't be there to hear them.

*

By the time Zach had arrived and they were all seated around a long table at the back of the restaurant, Jill decided that it was for the best that she hadn't told Becca about her ruse. It would have just put Becca in an awkward position tonight, when it was clear that she was already overwhelmed enough just being a part of it.

Frankie was seated to Jill's right, Carly and Nick across from them, and Zach at the end of the table.

The chair beside Jill was reserved for Becca, with Jonah at the head. The two had been hiding out in the kitchen while everyone else enjoyed the marinated olives and spiced nuts that had been put on the table along with a carefully selected bottle of wine.

"Now the question is are those two love birds back there cooking, or did they get distracted along the way?" Frankie joked.

Everyone laughed because they'd all been thinking it, Frankie was just the only one bold enough to say it aloud.

"It's nice seeing them back together," Jill said, knowing how difficult their breakup had been for Becca. She'd chosen to stay behind and work at the bakery rather than follow Jonah to California, thus ending their engagement. Jill had never asked her to stay behind, and at one point she'd even told her that it would be okay if she went, but like Jill, Becca felt a duty to the bakery.

More than that, she felt a connection. The bakery was their home. It was who they are.

And this restaurant was home to Jonah. It just took him a while to come back to it.

"Everything fell into place for the two of them," Carly agreed. "Just when they least expected it."

"The same could be said for the two of you," Nick said to Jill and Frankie, taking a sip of wine. "So tell us, how exactly did this all come about?"

Jill froze and darted a glance at Frankie. They hadn't gone over this, hadn't prepared for any questions. To do so would have felt deliberately deceitful, and that wasn't part of the bargain.

"Did I miss something here?" Zach's eyes darted over the table.

Jill felt her shoulders relax. Saved. For now.

"Frankie and Jill are dating," Carly informed Zach. She slid a glance at Jill, hiding her smile behind her wineglass.

"Frankie and…Jill?" Zach's surprise was so obvious that it would have been comical if Jill didn't feel a little insulted.

"Is that so hard to believe?" she asked, reaching for her water glass, hoping it might cool the heat in her cheeks.

Zach stared at them, blinking, his mouth still open. "Since when?"

Beside her, Frankie shrugged. "Oh, I don't know. A couple of weeks?"

She nodded. Everyone knew about the drinks they'd had at the Rustic Tavern, but were they going to imply that more had led up to that night?

More had, of course, but only they knew the details.

She shared a secret smile with him.

"And I'm just finding this out now?" Zach shot an accusatory look at Frankie. "I just saw you at the fire station last night."

"Yeah, well, it didn't come up," Frankie replied. "Besides, I assumed you'd know by now. My mother has pretty much told the entire town."

He laughed, and the rest of the table joined in. Everyone except for Zach, who still seemed to be processing this news.

Was it so hard for him to believe that Frankie might be interested in her?

Jill watched Frankie, admiring his ability to lighten a tense moment, but then, that was what he'd always done, as far back as their school days. He didn't let things bother him, at least not like she did. Even now, when her heart was pounding against her ribcage, he was coolly sipping his drink.

Jill glanced at Zach and felt her good spirits dwindle a little, reminding her of what people thought about her in town, and maybe even at this table. She'd never been the life of any party; she was far too reserved for that. Too sensible. Too practical.

Too responsible.

But that didn't mean she didn't enjoy a good time. And that was what she intended to do tonight.

"I hope everyone is hungry!" a voice called out and they all turned to see Jonah carrying a large tray of food, Becca following behind with a large bowl in each hand.

While Jonah and Becca set down the plates, Frankie leaned and whispered in Jill's ear, his warm breath sending a shiver down her spine. "Thanks for going along with it."

"Just doing my part," she reminded him, then, catching Carly's eye across the table, pulled herself away. If her sister had overheard their words, she didn't show it. If anything, she looked more pleased than usual.

Jonah explained the dishes, which all looked and smelled so wonderful that there was no doubt in Jill's mind about the taste, and from the broad smile on Becca's face, none for her either.

There was a salad of heirloom tomatoes and fresh burrata, a risotto made with seasonal produce and grilled shrimp, and a roasted chicken that brought up memories of cold winter nights spent in Nana's warm and cozy kitchen.

Nick lifted his glass. "To the chef!"

"To the happy couple!" Carly said, grinning at Becca and then sliding a glance at Jill.

"To the future!" Frankie said as they all tapped glasses.

Jill held up her glass and toasted to that. Because for the

first time in a long time, she felt like she, too, had something to look forward to.

But as for the other thing…the future was never certain. And she'd learned that a long time ago.

*

"So, Jonah," Frankie said, once they'd all passed around the dishes and served themselves. "Tell us about the inspiration behind your dishes."

"I should have warned you to go easy on him, Frankie!" Becca said.

"I don't need to! Everything is delicious."

When Jonah tipped his chin, Frankie's voice rose higher. "When have you ever known me to be anything but completely honest?"

Jill reached for her wineglass and took a long sip—no doubt avoiding saying something that she might regret.

"Thinking of leaving Concetti's to be a food critic?" Nick joked.

"I could never leave Concetti's," Frankie said gravely. Just thinking such a thing felt nothing short of blasphemous.

"Shh," Carly said, nudging Nick with her elbows. "Maria has ears everywhere."

Frankie laughed. It was true and he didn't take offense. He knew that everyone at this table loved his mother for the reasons he did; they appreciated her big personality and heart.

"This is a family restaurant," Jonah said, pausing to look around the room. "When my parents had their bistro in this space, it was where I learned to cook, where I saw that food didn't just fill the basic needs, it brought people together. A good meal could create a memory, and that's what I wanted to bring back to this room. The food will be served family style, just like we're eating tonight."

Frankie fell silent, letting that sink in, knowing just how true it was. Every time he prepared one of his father's recipes, he felt like he was ten years old again, still mastering the craft, trying to make the man proud.

Twenty years after his passing, he was still doing that.

"Interesting concept," Jill remarked. She looked at Becca. "You never told us that."

"This isn't my restaurant," Becca said. "It's Jonah's. And I wanted him to be the one to tell you."

"And show you!" Jonah grinned. "So, you think it will be a success?"

Everyone spoke at once in obvious agreement.

"Good thing you don't have too many Italian dishes on the menu or we might be in trouble," Frankie admitted.

The idea of family style was something that they'd never considered at Concetti's, but that didn't mean the food wasn't shared. How often did he see people trade a bit of their dish, and how many nights did he place two spoons beside one serving of tiramisu?

Jonah took pride in his work. It showed in each bite of the delicious food, perfectly seasoned, and carefully created, much like Mamma herself.

And once, Frankie's father.

As usual, when he thought of the man, he felt an ache rise in his throat. He reached for his wineglass to wash it down.

He wasn't the only one at this table to experience loss, Frankie knew, looking around at the Sunrise Sisters, and Jonah. They'd all found a way to carry on some part of their loved ones, to share the best parts of them.

Some maybe more so than others, he thought.

"Well, why don't I clear this away and bring out the dessert? I'm doing a sampling of several options, so I hope you saved room." Jonah and Becca both stood. "And feel free to walk around while you wait. It might take a few minutes."

Jill stood and walked across the room with Nick and Carly, who wanted to check out the bar area, leaving Frankie and Zach behind to finish the bottle of wine. No doubt, Jonah would be bringing a new one to pair with the next course.

"You and Jill Parker," Zach said, shaking his head. "I still can't wrap my head around it."

"You're saying you don't believe it?" Frankie asked Zach. He hadn't foreseen this, that someone would call their bluff, see through their little ruse.

Maybe that was because his interactions with Jill up until now had felt strangely realistic.

"What part don't you believe?" Jill asked, returning to her seat.

Frankie fought back a grin at Zach's expression, which seemed to struggle between disbelief and something closer to disappointment.

"Yeah, is it so hard to believe that a girl like Jill would put up with a chump like me?" Frankie joked and then, hoping that it wouldn't earn him an elbow in the ribs, he wrapped an arm over Jill's shoulder, surprised by how small it felt under his large palm.

He'd always seen Jill as a large force, almost like Mamma herself. A no-nonsense woman with a stiff upper lip and rigid habits. Now, as his fingers grazed her skin, he realized she was softer than he'd once believed.

For a moment, he felt her stiffen ever so slightly under his touch, but she didn't squirm away, or make up an excuse to get up again.

"It's just that you two are so different, that's all," Zach said.

"Oh, I wouldn't agree with you," Jill mused.

Frankie tried not to show his surprise. Anyone at this table knew that Jill was known for being serious and Frankie for anything but.

She was playing along, stepping in to defend their so-called relationship. But as he watched the little smile curve her mouth, he found himself believing her.

"We both love food and sharing it with the public. And we both understand the importance of working for a family business." She looked up at him. "Frankie's one of the most loyal guys I've ever met. And the most hard-working too."

Frankie's eyes locked with hers, and, remembering that they weren't alone at the table, he cleared his throat and glanced away.

"Sorry," Zach said. "I just...well, I'm surprised. That's all."

Frankie was growing tired of Zach's doubt and one glance at Jill confirmed that she wasn't exactly pleased by his words, either. Her smile had fallen into a small pout, and her blue eyes had gone a little flat.

Feeling his defenses rise, Frankie pulled Jill a little closer. "Maybe this will erase your doubts."

Frankie turned until he was facing her, so close that they were nearly nose to nose. He saw her eyes flash in panic on his for a moment, but she didn't swat him away, didn't come up with an excuse to run off and find one of her sisters.

Instead, her gaze locked on his, searching for an answer, for what his intentions were. For what he was about to do next, even though he hadn't planned it.

He leaned down and gently kissed her, her lips soft against his, not at all resistant. His groin tightened and he knew that he could have kept going, kissed her longer, pulled her closer, but that wouldn't be exactly appropriate.

And not just because they had an audience.

Jill wasn't his girlfriend. He wasn't even dating her.

But right here, right now, it sure as heck felt like he was.

*

"I hope that was okay back there," Frankie said the moment they were outside. Jonah and Becca remained in the restaurant, and Carly and Nick had stuck behind to help clean up. Zach had been the first to leave, claiming an early morning.

"Okay?" she remarked, fighting off a smile. "I can think of many words, and okay isn't one of them."

He could think of many words too, and as she'd said, okay wasn't one of them. That kiss had been brief, but its impact was lasting, staying with him now, making him think things that he'd never considered, want things he couldn't have.

Jill was just a friend. But that kiss... If he didn't know better, he'd say that there was something there. Chemistry, he supposed.

Or maybe…connection.

"What are you smiling about?" he asked, not so sure if she was pleased or amused.

"Oh, that comment you made a while back, about what a good kisser you are," she said vaguely.

He stared at her, waiting for her to confirm his reputation, but instead, she just swung her handbag and kept walking.

"So, you're just going to leave me hanging like that?" he said, catching up to her.

"You'd better be happy that I was well-fed tonight, or I might have reacted a little differently," was all she said.

"Ah, so I'm not the only one who never likes to skip a meal. Another thing in common then." He paused, studying her. "Did you mean what you said to Zach? About what we had in common?"

"Sure," she said with a casual shrug. "You don't agree?"

"I do," he said quickly. "I definitely do. I just…never thought about it before."

Never thought of a lot of things before.

He glanced down at the pretty sundress she wore, the long legs that walked with purpose, like she knew where she was going, even though right now, he didn't have a clue what was happening between them. He just knew that something had shifted. Or maybe, opened.

"Is that a good thing or a bad thing?" he asked, trying to answer the question for himself and coming up blank. He liked Jill. Always had. As the girl he thought she was. But now, she felt different somehow.

She gave him a funny look and stopped when she'd reached her car door, where they'd part for the night. "I'm not so sure."

He nodded. Because neither was he.

chapter eleven

As much as Jill hated the thought of leaving Toffee for a few hours on Sunday afternoon, she knew that if she wanted to get a dress for the wedding, this was likely her only chance.

And if she chose wisely, she could also wear it to Nana's upcoming birthday party. It made a handy excuse when Carly asked what had prompted Jill's sudden interest in a shopping day.

"We all want Nana's birthday to be special," Jill said as they walked around a boutique in Mapleton, stopping every few feet to consider an item.

"Speaking of which," Carly stopped to look at her. "We still haven't received an entry from Concetti's for the cookbook. Our deadline to collect everything is next Sunday if we want to get the book printed in time."

"Don't worry," Jill said as she picked up a pair of

earrings and held them to her lobe. Compared to her usual pearl studs, they seemed large and impractical. "Frankie's giving me the recipe for their sauce."

Carly's eyes went wide. "Their pizza sauce?"

Jill returned the earrings to the table. "We did ask everyone to contribute their best recipe."

"Still." Carly seemed to take a moment to digest this information. "That's quite a feat! How'd you manage that?"

If only you knew, Jill thought, moving on to another table, this one containing bracelets and silk scarves, nothing she needed, and certainly not the purpose of this trip.

"I guess he likes you…"

"More like he knows that this benefits the fire department," Jill corrected her sister, reminding herself of what were most likely Frankie's true reasons for agreeing to share the recipe.

Along with the wedding date.

"What about this dress?" Jill held up a simple navy sheath dress with spaghetti straps.

"I like it!" Carly nodded in approval. "And it would look nice with those earrings you were just looking at."

"It will look just as good with my pearls," Jill said, looking at the dress more closely.

"You mean your everyday earrings?" Carly tsked her disapproval. "This is a party, Jill. Not everything has to be so practical."

Jill felt her heart speed up a little. She'd dared to act a little impulsively lately, to listen to her heart instead of her head, and she'd be the first to admit that she felt better than she had in years.

"Okay," she said, laughing.

"Go try it on!" Carly said, motioning toward the dressing rooms. "I'll look for matching shoes. If we don't find any, I have gold strappy heels you can borrow."

"Thanks, Carly," Jill said, meaning it.

"There's nothing to thank me for!" Carly smiled brightly but then hesitated, letting her fingers graze the fringe on a sweater. "It...meant a lot to me that you asked me to come shopping with you today. I mean, sure we see each other at the bakery every day, and we have our dinners with Nana, but that's different. I've always wanted this kind of relationship with you."

The sparkle had left Carly's eyes and in its place, Jill saw something else. Hurt, maybe, and certainly a feeling that Jill had never intended to cause.

"I had no idea you felt that way," Jill said softly. She swallowed against her own building emotions. "The bakery has always taken up so much of my time..."

Carly nodded. "I know. And I know how much it means to you, Jill. And I'm not upset with you about that. If anything, I feel like I'm the one who should be thanking you."

"Me?" Jill stared at her sister, realizing that it had been a long time since they'd communicated like this. Their usual conversations were covered in banter or focused on the bakery—their common bond.

But they were sisters. Sisters who had grown apart over the years when Carly moved away, but now Jill didn't have an excuse for keeping Carly at arm's length anymore. Her little sister was all grown up, with a boyfriend and his daughter to consider, and she'd given more back to the bakery than just her time. Her ideas were good ones. In the bakery, and outside of it, too.

"I mean, you're the one who kept the place going when I went to college," Carly said.

"Becca and Nana were there too," Jill pointed out.

"I know, but you've always taken on the brunt of the responsibility. Ever since Mom died. And I don't just mean at the bakery." Carly's eyes turned soft, and Jill could only nod. "But now I'm back, and a full partner at the bakery, and I don't want you to feel like it's all on you. We all share the responsibility now."

Jill hesitated. She knew it was true, and it was what both of her sisters kept telling her, too. But somehow, she couldn't bring herself to release her hold on the business any more than relinquish some of her responsibility for it.

Or her sisters.

But now, looking at her baby sister, all grown up, and advising her, Jill realized that she didn't have to take care of everything on her own anymore. If she was willing to give up a little control in exchange for letting Carly in.

"I guess I've just grown used to feeling like I have to take care of everything," she admitted.

"But I want to help more," Carly insisted. "Then maybe we can have more days like this. I want you to feel less stressed so that you can let a little fun in."

"Is that why you're always encouraging me to date?" Jill asked, sensing there was more to Carly's insistence.

"I'd be lying if I said it wouldn't lessen my conscience if you got out a little bit, let me shoulder some of the work at the bakery. Sometimes…" Carly shook her head as if re-considering her words.

"No," Jill said, setting a hand on her sister's wrist. "I want to hear it."

"Sometimes I feel like I'm not a full partner. Like you're holding on so tight to the bakery because you assume I'll mess everything up or leave town again."

Jill stared at her sister. Sure, there were times when she didn't think that Carly took the bakery very seriously, but those days were in the past, along, Jill realized, with so many other things.

"Carly, if you hadn't come back to town last spring, we might have lost the bakery. You know that I appreciate you, don't you?"

Carly nodded, but she didn't look completely convinced.

"And you're madly in love with Nick and his daughter," Jill told her. "It never even crossed my mind that you'd leave town again."

"Then why hold on to the bakery so tightly?" Carly asked. "Why not share the work with Becca and me? We're equal in this, Jill. Aren't we?"

"We are," Jill told her firmly, feeling bad it had ever come across any other way. She shook her head, looking around the boutique, which was filled with beautiful things, items waiting to be discovered, tried on, or just enjoyed on a too-rare shopping trip, like today. It had been years since Jill had properly gone clothes shopping, certainly not with one of her sisters, and certainly not for something just for fun. Something frivolous. Something pretty. Something that didn't serve any purpose other than to bring a smile to her face.

"I guess I've just grown used to my routine," she said. "I'm sorry, Carly. For making you feel excluded from the business. For not making more time for moments like this."

"Well, today can be the first of many," Carly said with that cheeky grin that Jill had seen all of her life. "After all, you'll have lots of dates to shop for…"

And they were back on the subject of dating. Jill laughed but there was a little pain in her heart when she thought of the secret that she was keeping from her sister.

Carly just wanted the best for her. And more than that—she wanted a relationship with her. Jill closed the door to the dressing room and looked at herself in the mirror, wondering where the years had gone. How easily she'd let them slip by, each day, week, and month the same.

Until now.

She'd thought she was holding on to what mattered most—the bakery, the traditions that were so important to her family.

But she'd ended up pushing away one of the people that meant the most to her in the process, shutting out the present along with the past. And maybe, almost, even the future.

*

Jill wasn't surprised when Maria popped into the bakery on Tuesday. Her presence at the bakery wasn't rare, but her motive for being there today was no doubt ulterior.

"Good morning, Maria!" Jill said cheerfully. "What can I get you for this morning?"

"I had a taste for one of those blueberry muffins if there are any left." Maria craned her neck to study the pastry case where Jill knew the blueberry muffins were hiding behind their raspberry counterparts.

Just to be sure, she doubled-checked and plated the last of the batch.

"There you go," she said, sliding the plate to Maria, who she knew liked to stay and relax and enjoy her food and coffee rather than take anything to go. "Would you like some coffee with that?"

"Please," Maria said, eyeing her suggestively. After a brief hesitation, she added, "I ran into your grandmother yesterday."

"Oh?" Jill kept her tone politely disinterested, even though what she was really thinking was, *Oh great*. It was inevitable that Nana would hear about her so-called dating Frankie, but she'd rather it hadn't come directly from Frankie's mother.

No doubt those two were already tossing around potential dates for a Parker-Concetti wedding.

"She told me about her birthday party," Maria said. She tapped on the sign that was still propped up on the counter.

"Oh!" Now Jill was happy to engage. "Yes, and I hope that you haven't told her about the gift. It's a big surprise."

"I didn't, because this is the first I'm hearing of it!" Maria frowned at her. "Is this something I should have known?"

Jill immediately felt bad for the oversight. She'd talked

to Frankie instead of Maria without considering that the two hadn't communicated amongst themselves.

"Well, the idea started small and then sort of grew into something of its own," Jill said. "We had the idea to do a special cookbook for Nana, full of recipes from all of her closest friends in town."

"What a lovely idea!" Maria said. "I'd be happy to participate, of course."

"Well," Jill warned. "We then considered how there's only one thing that my grandmother loves more than sharing her cherished recipes with those that she loves. This community means everything to her, and so we decided to make it a community cookbook. She'll get the first copy, as her gift, but then we'll put it up for sale, here in the bakery. The proceeds will go to the fire station."

"That's a wonderful idea!" Maria's expression folded into one of confusion. "But I can't believe that Frankie never told me. Especially given that the proceeds go to the fire department."

"Oh, he's probably just been busy," Jill said, instantly regretting her words when she saw the suggestive lift of Maria's eyebrows.

"He certainly has!" She gave a coy smile. "Well, I suppose I can't stay mad at him, then. Not that I ever can."

Jill hesitated, wondering where the conversation would lead if she told Maria it was because she'd already asked Frankie, and how Maria would feel about the recipe Frankie promised to contribute, when Maria straightened her shoulders.

"Everyone will want to contribute their best recipe, I suppose! Put me down for my famous sauce, dear."

Jill stared at Maria, wondering if she'd misheard, and forgot all about the coffee she was pouring until it spilled over the rim of the mug onto her fingers.

Wincing, she snatched her hand back and wiped it on her apron.

"Your *pizza* sauce?" she said slowly.

"Everyone loves it!" Maria said, nodding. "I can't think of a better contribution, can you?"

Jill didn't know what to make of this. Why Maria was so willing to hand it over and why Frankie was so resistant to part with it?

Had it all been a ploy to get her to play along with this date? Had he known that his mother would freely give it all along?

"I wasn't sure if that was a secret family recipe," she said carefully, sliding the mug across the counter to Maria.

Maria's smile turned wistful for a moment. "Oh, a special family recipe. Secret, perhaps. But not in a competitive way. Life is short. And like food, it's meant to be enjoyed and shared. If you keep all the best parts of yourself to yourself, you'll end up very lonely indeed."

Indeed, Jill thought, her mind wandering to Carly's confession on Sunday at the shop. She'd tried to hold on so tight to this bakery, that she'd inadvertently tried to push her sister out.

"I'll email that recipe to you tonight," Maria said, taking down the information. Then, giving a more suggestive smile, she said, "And I'll see *you* on Saturday!"

Saturday. The time had snuck up on her, and Jill couldn't help but think that all too soon this ruse would come to an end, just when she'd started to get used to it.

*

Usually, Jill was greeted by the sound of Toffee when she returned home, but today, when she turned the key in the door, she heard nothing.

She paused, waiting for the sound that had become so easily familiar, but it didn't come. Smiling to herself, she considered that maybe he'd finally gotten used to his little den, or maybe fallen asleep after a good, long walk, but when she called his name and he still didn't answer, her heart sped up with panic.

She hurried to the back of the house, her heart seizing up in her chest when she saw that the gate was open, the room empty.

Immediately, she searched the kitchen, scanning her eyes to the back door, relieved to see that it was closed, then moved into the living room, calling her puppy's name with increasing anxiety. She kept a tidy house—or at least she had until Toffee came into her life and left his toys wherever he'd last played with them—but there were still several ways he could get into mischief.

And worse: trouble.

"Toffee?" She ran into the backyard, even though she didn't see how he couldn't have gotten outside unless Frankie had forgotten to bring him in—the mere thought of this made her heart pound against her ribcage and she scanned the yard, seeing nothing, swinging her focus to the gate, which was still latched.

"Toffee?" She darted back into the kitchen, only to see his tiny form sprinting toward her. Relief flooded her as she scooped him into her arms and held him close, waiting for her pulse to come down.

Frankie appeared around the corner, looking at her in confusion. "You look scared to death."

"I couldn't find Toffee," she explained, still a little out of breath.

"I took him for a later walk than usual," Frankie explained. Then, sensing her panic, his expression turned to one of concern. "Jill, he was fine. I was with him the entire time."

"I know." She told herself that it was true, that everything was fine, but something had been awakened in her just now. An emotion she hadn't experienced in a long time. One that she'd tried to forget.

One that she'd protected herself from.

And she recognized it now for what it was. Fear. And not just fear, but the worst kind of fear. Fear of losing someone she loved very much.

For these past two weeks since Toffee had come into her life, she had only focused on the joy he'd brought to her, and now, she realized that he hadn't just filled a part of her heart, he'd also opened it up. To love. But also the prospect of loss.

She swallowed hard and paced the kitchen.

"I'm sorry, Jill. If I'd known you were coming home so early, I would have left a note," Frankie said, his brow creased with worry.

"No, it's fine." Jill took a deep breath and set Toffee on the floor to get some water from his bowl. "I just…I didn't know where he was."

Frankie gave her a lopsided grin. "You love the little guy, don't you?"

"More than I thought was possible," she said honestly.

"That's a beautiful thing," he told her.

She nodded. "Scary too. At the thought of…" She shook her head. She didn't want to think about it, imagine it, or even plan for it. Because that was the problem with loss, wasn't it? Nothing you could do could stop it. Delay it, maybe. But she'd been fooling herself to ever think that she might be able to control her world, keep everything and everyone she loved forever.

Frankie set a hand on her shoulder. "Hey, he's safe. He's fine. Why don't you let me pour you a glass of wine?"

He opened her fridge, retrieving a bottle of white wine that had been chilling there for a couple of weeks since Becca had moved out.

"Stay and have a glass with me," Jill offered out of politeness until she felt the pull in her chest as she waited for his answer. There was a part of her that wanted Frankie to stay. To keep her company. Make her laugh.

But the other part of her thought it would be best if he left. Let her get back to her evening. Knowing that come Sunday, these moments would also come to a sudden end.

"Sure," he said easily, reaching for another glass. "It's a nice night. We can sit out back and let Toffee play on the grass." He paused to give her a pointed look. "That is if you think your fully fenced-in backyard is a safe place for him. Or should I get his leash?"

Jill laughed and swatted Frankie's arm playfully. "I'm not that uptight. Not like you think I am. I just…worry. I like to feel…prepared."

"I get it," Frankie said as his expression sobered. "If

you're always one step ahead of the problems, it feels like they'll never really catch up to you."

Jill thought about that as they stepped outside and settled onto the small patio table set, her chair facing the yard, giving her a full view of every angle. Toffee wasted no time in dashing from one side to the next, and his energy made her smile, relaxing her.

He certainly knew how to live life to its fullest.

Jill felt Frankie's eyes on her and sighed, feeling the need to explain her earlier panic.

"I guess I've always tried to minimize potential worry," she said. Or pain.

"How's that working out for you?" Frankie asked, his tone implying that he already knew the answer.

Jill glanced at him, knowing he had her there. "Not great," she admitted. Not when she thought about what her sister had told her at the boutique.

"Growing up, it was easier. After my mother got sick and then passed away, I found a purpose in focusing on my sisters and my grandmother. I guess I was scared that something could happen to one of them, too. That if I kept an eye on them, did everything I was supposed to, made sure that everything was accounted for and taken care of, that if I did my work and did it well, and filled every hour of the day with purpose, that somehow, there wouldn't be any room for disaster."

She swallowed against the lump in her throat, thinking back on those days. The comfort she took in making sure that her grandmother wasn't overworked at the bakery, that she could alleviate some of that stress, that she could make sure that her sisters still at least had the one place that had brought them so many happy memories. That she could keep the bakery, even if she couldn't keep her mother.

Until she'd almost lost it.

"I was the one who forced my grandmother to retire," she told Frankie. "Her arthritis had been bad for a long time and I could see that she was struggling. And I also knew that she'd never admit that she needed help."

"Sounds like someone I know." Frankie raised an eyebrow.

Jill gave a small smile. "It made me feel even more obligated to the bakery. I had to keep it going for her. Especially when I was the one who encouraged her to leave. But then when she left, people stopped coming in, and no matter how much I tried to keep everything exactly the same, it didn't matter." She still felt tense thinking of those long days and sleepless nights, the way she'd agonized over replicating Nana's recipes only to find that no one wanted to come in and buy them.

"I know the bakery had its struggles last year, but now look at the place! Never looked better!" Frankie raised his glass.

Jill nodded. "It's true. But that's all Carly's doing. The truth is that if she hadn't come back to town and made us consider some changes to the menu and the ambiance, I'm not sure we'd still have a business. People weren't coming in for Nana's old-fashioned recipes. They were coming for Nana."

"She's a special person," Frankie said with a small smile.

"But I don't think you're giving yourself enough credit. You chose to implement Carly's ideas instead of turning them down. You've never failed at anything in your life, Jill."

Jill thought about this, knowing that once it might have been true, but not anymore. She'd failed her sister, after all.

"I know you, Jill," Frankie said, leaning forward across the table. "You would have found a way to save that bakery. When something means that much, you don't let it go."

No, you don't. And that brought Jill back to what had happened today, with Maria being so willing to hand over a recipe that Frankie couldn't seem to part with.

"Can I ask you something?" Jill asked, studying his face. "Why are you so unwilling to share that recipe?"

"Well, lots of restaurants have secret recipes," Frankie pointed out after a pause. He looked tense now as he reached for his wineglass.

It was true, and Nana had fallen into that trap for a while, too, but she knew this wasn't the case with Concetti's.

"If we go giving away our secrets, no one would come," Frankie added.

"Oh, I don't think so at all," Jill disagreed. "Look at all the cookbooks out there, several from famous restaurants and chefs. If you give people a taste of what you can offer, you might only make people want to come to the restaurant all the more."

Frankie conceded with a shrug before taking another sip of wine.

"And I'm not under the impression that Concetti's has

ever been hurting for business," Jill said, hoping that she was right.

"No, we've been lucky, which is why I don't want to tempt it," Frankie said. But there was a worrying frown on his face that told Jill there was much more to it.

Jill brushed away his concern. "There was a time when I held on to Nana's recipes, too. I didn't want to share them, only bake them, and I didn't want to even think about deviating from tradition. I could recreate her recipes in my sleep. Sometimes, I actually did." Jill started to laugh. "Sleepwalking. It was something I did when I was younger. Stress, I suppose. After my mother died."

She fell silent, looking up at Frankie when he set a warm hand on her wrist.

"It's not easy to lose a parent," he said, his dark eyes full of sympathy—and not just that, but also, understanding.

"No," Jill said, shaking her head as much as she tried to shake away the hurt in her chest. "It's not. And I think that's why the thought of losing the bakery too was so upsetting for me. I poured my entire life into that place." Leaving very little room for anything—or anyone—else.

"It's easy to hold on to people and memories and things that were important to you. You asked me about the recipe, and the truth is that it was special to me." Frankie grinned, looking wistful. "Every Sunday my dad and I would go into the kitchen and make that sauce, enough to last for a week. It's actually a really simple recipe, but there was something about being with him in that kitchen, just the two of us, that I looked forward to every week. It wasn't on the calendar, but it was something certain in my life. Until it wasn't."

Jill gave him a sad smile. "Every time I smell my mother's favorite cookies, I feel like she's right there in the room, with me again. I guess if someone wanted to take that recipe and spread it around town, I wouldn't be very willing to share it. It's different when I'm the one doing the baking and the sharing."

"So you were right then," he said as his dark gaze locked on hers. "We do have a lot in common."

She hesitated, wondering if she should tell him about what happened. That if she went and checked her email right now, she might have the recipe waiting in her inbox. That there'd be no reason to continue this ruse. That their deal was over.

But instead, she thought about how quickly he'd refused to share it. How important it was to him to hold on to it, keep it close.

Maybe she was right. She and Frankie did have a lot in common. Certainly, more than she'd ever known.

chapter twelve

Frankie wasn't surprised when all the guys at the station whistled when he dropped off two trays of pasta on Saturday afternoon, already dressed in his best suit and tie, the last stop before he picked up Jill and braced himself for what was sure to be a long night ahead.

"Frankie, you clean up nicely!" Zach said, coming to help him carry the boxes. Then, with a little smirk, he added, "You'd better be careful that you don't get any sauce on that suit or your mother might ground you and not let you go to the school dance."

"Yeah, yeah." Frankie knew that Zach was joking and that he, like most people in town, got a rise out of Mamma's overbearing nature.

But sometimes, it hit home, and today, with the wedding now only an hour away, Frankie wasn't in a laughing mood.

"It's a wedding, actually," Frankie added. "And you should be careful what you say or I might just take this food back to Concetti's."

Zach didn't seem to take offense either, but it was clear he had something to say as they set up the food on the table. Frankie was supposed to have been on shift tonight, and even though it wasn't a big deal that he was taking the evening off for a family event, he knew the guys would be counting on a home-cooked meal.

Frankie never liked to let people down. Not the guys here. Not Mamma. Maybe, that was the problem. It had certainly invited trouble, and today was a glaring example of that.

His stomach burned every time he thought about the position he had put Jill in—asking her to pose as his date, knowing how his family members could be. They'd do more than shoot her glances. They'd do more than introduce themselves. They'd want details. Information.

Probably, a wedding date. Or at least a ring size.

And if he thought he'd have trouble handling his own family today, how did he expect Jill to be able to do it?

"You bringing a date?" Zach's tone, while casual, didn't match the strange expression on his face. He focused on the food, not making eye contact, and all joking had officially stopped.

"I'm bringing Jill," Frankie replied. Then, because he still couldn't get Friday night out of his head, he said, "I'm sure that surprises you."

"I didn't mean any offense the other night, man." Zach looked at him sharply now. "To be honest, I think you're a lucky guy."

A Wish Come True

Frankie frowned at Zach, waiting for the punchline, knowing a jokester when he saw one, but now, like last Friday, Zach just seemed deflated.

"Why is it such a big deal to you that I've been spending time with Jill?" Frankie asked.

"I guess you could say I had a thing for her once," Zach said with a shrug.

"Jill?" Now Frankie was the one feeling shocked. Not that Jill wouldn't catch someone's eye, but that Zach had never done anything about it. "You date around. Why'd you never ask her out?"

"Because of what you said," Zach replied. "I date around. I haven't been looking to settle down. And Jill's the kind of girl you take seriously."

Frankie grew quiet. Zach was right—she wasn't the kind of girl you dated casually or just for fun.

"You snooze you lose, as the saying goes." Zach shrugged, but it was clear by the way he couldn't look Frankie in the eye that he meant every word that he'd said.

"Well, I should probably head out," Frankie said, feeling uneasy with the direction of this conversation. "My mother will legitimately punish me if I'm late to my cousin's wedding."

He cracked a smile, showing that there were no hurt feelings, and Zach did the same, but as Frankie walked back to his car, and started the drive to Jill's cottage, the only feelings he was thinking about were his own.

Zach liked Jill. Had for some time. More than that, he'd baited his time, waiting for the right moment to ask her out. When he was serious. Because she was a serious girl.

Just not in the way that Frankie had ever thought of her.

He pulled up to a stop outside of Jill's cottage and stepped out of the car. There was no sound of a barking dog when he knocked on her door, meaning that Jill had successfully trained Toffee since yesterday when Frankie stopped by to walk him again, or that the little dog was staying at one of her sisters' houses for the evening.

The door opened, and Jill stood on the other side, wearing a dark blue dress and sparkling earrings that brought out the depth of her light blue eyes. Her honey blond hair was swept up, but not severely like it was at the bakery. Or all the other times he saw her—or thought of her.

Only that wasn't true anymore, was it? Now, when he thought of Jill, he pictured her laughing with Toffee, or looking up at him with a smile in her eyes when her little dog did something sweet.

It was the kind of image he could hold on to...maybe even forever.

*

The last wedding that Jill had been to was her grandmother's unexpected marriage to Robert Quincy, otherwise known as Jonah's grandfather. For a large guestlist, it had been a surprisingly intimate ceremony and reception, seeing as everyone invited was so emotionally invested in the happy couple.

This wedding, Jill could already tell, was going to be a much bigger affair.

"You didn't think you could have just blended into the crowd?" Jill asked Frankie as they entered the large church.

Every row was packed with guests, and Jill wasn't even sure that they'd be able to find a seat.

Mamma Maria, however, had made sure that wouldn't happen.

In a bright pink dress that made it impossible not to spot her, she waved to them from the very front of the church, beckoning them forward. Two women who must have been her sisters turned and stared at them, and beside her, Jill felt Frankie stiffen.

"Never mind that comment. I can see now that wouldn't be possible." Jill smoothed the skirt of the navy dress she'd purchased at the shop in Mapleton last weekend. With Carly's borrowed strappy heels, the look came together easily, and even Jill had to admit that she was happy she bought the earrings, too.

There was something to be said for stepping outside her comfort zone, but today, she was starting to wish that she'd stayed home.

"I'm sorry about the scrutiny," Frankie said.

"I can only begin to imagine what your mother has told them," Jill said, regretting going along with this ruse. She never liked being the center of attention, preferring instead to stay out of the spotlight, at home, or in the kitchen bakery where her world was contained and controlled.

Frankie seemed to share her apprehension when he adjusted the collar of his shirt, his jaw set as he stared out into the sea of onlookers.

"They'll shift their attention on the bride and groom soon enough," he assured her.

Jill wasn't so sure of that, and from the looks of it, Frankie wasn't either. Still, they'd come this far.

"I guess there's no turning back now," she said.

"Thinking about the recipe you get at the end of the night?" Frankie glanced at her.

Jill hesitated, knowing that right now, the recipe was the least of her worries, especially since, as promised, Maria had emailed it to her Tuesday evening. It was compiled with all the other contributions, waiting to go to the printer on Monday.

"Don't worry," Frankie said before she could speak up. "You'll have earned it after tonight. Should we get this over with?"

Frankie extended his elbow and Jill saw no other choice than to take it, finding a strange sense of comfort in doing so, and not just because of his sturdy build. There may be rows of strangers staring at her, but Frankie was familiar. More than that—he always had her back.

She smiled as they walked down the aisle, feeling the wide eyes on her with every step, until they finally scooted into the row beside Maria, who looked pleased as punch when she glanced at her sisters.

Jill had of course seen Frankie's various cousins who occasionally helped out at Concetti's, but she had never met Maria's sisters, who, probably like the mother of the bride who was yet to make her appearance, all bore a striking resemblance in their facial structure—though right now, the most obvious shared trait was the hope in their eyes.

Jill's stomach tightened with guilt as she slid into the pew and took her seat beside Frankie, who was wedged between her and his mother. He stared straight ahead, trying to ignore his gleeful aunts and boasting mother, until the music swelled and the procession began, turning everyone's attention to the aisle.

As Frankie promised, once the ceremony was underway, his mother and aunts did put their attention where it belonged, aside from a few telltale glances. Jill sat and watched as the bride and groom took their vows and sealed them with a kiss, and when the happy couple turned and smiled out onto the guests who had come to support them, she felt the pull of someone's eyes on her.

Against her better judgment, she glanced to her left, expecting to meet Mamma Maria's suggestive stare, but instead, her gaze met Frankie's.

She swallowed hard against the sudden pounding in her chest and gave him a little smile before turning away, standing with the rest of the guests, who were eager to file out of the church and get to the reception where wine would be flowing and no doubt delicious food would be served.

The wedding was over. All that was left for the night was the party.

And soon all of this would just be another part of her past.

*

If Jill thought that she'd gotten the worst part of the day over with at the wedding ceremony, it paled in comparison to the reception that was held in the private garden next door.

Even though Frankie had made a point of getting lost in the crowd exiting the church, somehow Maria and her sisters were already stationed near a cocktail table by the time Frankie and Jill had nabbed their first glass of champagne from a passing waiter.

"Frankie," Maria said, coming up to them. "Why don't you introduce your lovely date to everyone?"

"Of course." Frankie slid Jill a wide-eyed look and then made the introductions.

All the women seemed as pleased as Mamma Maria that Jill was there, and none of them were shy in asking questions either.

"Did you two just meet?" the sister named Elena asked.

Jill glanced at Frankie, who seemed weary by the questions. Jill reminded herself that even though she was just stepping into this conversation, Frankie had probably been having some form of it for years.

"We grew up together," Jill explained. "I guess you could say we've known each other all our lives."

Even though she was starting to feel like she never really knew him at all.

"I couldn't be happier that you were able to join us today," the mother of the bride, Diana, said before excusing herself to stand for photos with the wedding party.

"I know someone happier," the sister named Angela chided. She waggled a finger at Maria. "And here we thought you'd be crying instead of clapping at this wedding, Maria!"

"Oh." Maria brushed away their concern. "You know I would never meddle in my son's personal life."

Now Jill had to push back a laugh, covering her smile by taking a sip from her glass.

"If you don't mind excusing us," Frankie said, slipping a hand around her waist. "I'd like to enjoy my date's company for a bit."

Jill stiffened against the sensation of his large hand near her hip, the way it lingered there, like a warm, reassuring weight. And even though she knew he was just hamming it up for his aunts, she couldn't help but feel a pull toward him, a connection that went beyond the ruse they were, rather successfully, pulling off.

"I feel like I owe you more than a recipe after that," Frankie said, loosening his tie as they found their table, where they were seated with some of Frankie's cousins and their spouses, who, unlike their mothers, didn't seem as concerned about Frankie's love life or choice of date.

The dinner was easy enough to get through, with the speeches taking up most of the attention, leaving Jill and Frankie to enjoy their food without too many questions about the nature of their relationship. And aside from a few glances across the yard from Maria, no one paid them much attention.

For a moment, Jill thought that the night hadn't been nearly as stressful as Frankie had implied it would be until everyone started to rise from the table and one of Frankie's other female cousins approached.

"Frankie," she said, giving him a funny look. "This is my friend Bianca."

A woman with long, curly brown hair and a figure that Jill could never hope to obtain by working in a bakery every day of her life gave Frankie the full once-over with her striking green eyes.

"Ah, yes, your aunts told me all about you, Frankie," she said, extending a hand.

Frankie looked uneasy as he shook it. "I can only imagine what you've heard," he replied.

"Oh, all good things," Bianca replied with a little curl of her lip. She gave Jill a fleeting glance, as if just now noticing her, and then gave a little shrug to Frankie before walking away with his cousin at her side.

"Let me guess," Jill said. "One of the women your mother had invited to set you up with?"

"And if there's one, there will be others." Frankie didn't look pleased as he watched the woman walk away, her stride effortless even in her stiletto heels on the uneven grass.

"She seemed very nice," Jill said, feeling bad that the words were forced.

Bianca had seemed perfectly nice. Perfectly beautiful too. There was no doubt that she would have easily caught Frankie's interest, and still might.

Jill looked up at him, wondering if he had any doubts— about bringing her instead of leaving the door open to new possibilities.

"I'm sure she is," was all Frankie said. "All the women I've dated have been perfectly nice. But none of them last very long."

"You sound defeated," Jill said, echoing the feeling. She'd worn a new dress for today, and new shoes, too, which were now digging into her heels and giving her blisters. She didn't know what she'd exactly hoped would happen today, but this wasn't it. Beautiful, single women at every turn. When her fake relationship with Frankie ended, he'd have his pick of dates.

This was their bargain. She should be happy that she'd seen it through, that she'd gotten what she'd wanted from it.

But she couldn't help but feel that she'd found more than she'd wanted.

"My mother thinks I'm too picky," Frankie said, grabbing two glasses of wine from a tray. He handed her one. "I know what you're thinking."

"I didn't say a word," Jill replied, but she hid her smile behind her glass. Maria was known to find fault with several of the women that Frankie dated.

"Maybe I've been trying too hard." But Frankie didn't look completely convinced by his own words. "I date. A lot. But…" He shrugged as if he didn't know the answer to why none of those dates had led to anything more.

"You think you're too selective?" Jill asked. She'd seen plenty of women on Frankie's arm over the years, and each was as pretty as the next. They all seemed perfectly nice, too, but just as quickly as one came along, she was replaced with a similar model.

Jill eyed Bianca through the crowd. Bianca was Frankie's type. She fit the mold.

And Jill, despite the dress and the earrings and the shoes that hurt her feet, did not.

Frankie frowned as he considered her question and then shook his head. "No. Maybe I'm not selective enough. Or maybe I just haven't known what to look for."

He held her gaze for a beat until she felt her cheeks flush.

It was ridiculous to think that Frankie was referring to her. They were friends. After the past couple of weeks, she might even say good friends. Friends with more in common than she ever would have believed.

Than she'd ever given him a chance to share.

"Everyone's starting to dance," Frankie said, gesturing to the dance floor, where sure enough, couples were already swaying to the music in each other's arms. He didn't say more but just raised his eyebrows in question.

"Wait," she said, feeling herself tense up. "You didn't say dancing would be part of the deal."

"It's a wedding. Everyone dances at weddings!" He gave her one of those grins that flashed his dimples, the kind of smile that easily would have won the heart of any single girl at this wedding.

But it wasn't enough for Jill. She hadn't even danced at her grandmother's wedding this past summer.

Looking around, she realized that most people did dance at weddings, and today she had no excuse to sit at a table and be a spectator. Maria was already in the middle of the floor, clapping her hands and getting her sisters to join in.

She looked so radiant, that it almost seemed impossible to believe that she could have ever been upset about this wedding.

But then Jill looked up at Frankie, who wasn't looking at his mother, but who was instead watching her, and she knew the reason for Maria's joy.

For one night, she thought her son was fulfilled. Happy. Maybe even settled.

And who was Jill to take that away from her any sooner than she had to?

"I guess your mother will be expecting us to dance," Jill said nervously.

"You really don't like to dance, do you?" Frankie peered at her.

Jill shrugged, trying to slough off her unease. "I don't have much practice."

Frankie narrowed his eyes in thought. "I never saw you at the school dances."

"Oh, I was there," Jill said, begrudgingly. "Only because Becca always made me go, and Nana pulled the oldest sister card, convincing me that I had to keep an eye on Becca, even though she could hold her own." She glanced up at him and explained. "I would hide in the bathroom."

"Why?" he asked, his expression as incredulous as his tone. "Dances were fun!"

"Not for me," Jill said, shaking her head. Just thinking back on the apprehension she felt on those nights made her stomach clench all these years later.

"Why?" He gave her a look of exaggerated disappointment. "Were you afraid no one would ask you to dance?"

Jill hesitated. "I think that I was more afraid that they would."

"Okay, now you've lost me," Frankie said.

"I guess that I didn't want to get close to anyone after my mother died."

She waited for Frankie to crack a joke, something about how the high school bathroom couldn't have been more interesting than the decorated gymnasium, but instead, his dark eyes bored into hers as the silence stretched between them.

"Another thing we have in common then," he said softly.

"You? But you take life in stride," Jill said, looking at him in surprise. "Even after…"

"After my father died?" Frankie shook his head. "Hardly."

"But…you're the happiest person I know. You're always laughing, joking, even back then." Then. Now. Frankie was like Toffee. Living life to the fullest. Helping the community, working for the family business, and still making time for an active social life. And a dating life.

Always smiling. Always laughing.

"Sometimes it's easier to laugh than to cry," Frankie said, giving her a long look. "I made a promise to my father to keep my mother happy. I had to put on a brave face for her."

Jill's mouth tugged into a small smile. "More and more in common."

"I saw how sad she was, even when she didn't say it. And I saw how sad you were, too," Frankie said softly.

"You did?" Jill gasped. "But…" She'd tried so hard to hide it. To be strong. To take care of her sisters. Her grandmother. The bakery. Everything.

"That's why I always joked around with you," Frankie said. "I guess I liked seeing you smile. Just for a minute."

"And here I thought it was because I was so serious that you liked the challenge," she said.

"Well, that too," Frankie said with his old grin.

Jill blew out a sigh. "I guess I never realized that someone saw through my shell."

Frankie looked down at her now, his eyes soft, tender. "I don't think I'm the only one."

"What does that mean?" Jill asked, slightly alarmed.

But Frankie gave her an easy smile. "Just that there probably would have been guys lined up to dance with you if you'd ever come out of that bathroom."

Jill felt her cheeks flush, even though he was probably just being nice. Because that's what Frankie was. Nice. Kind. Helpful. Safe.

But he was more than that, she knew. Because now, looking up at him, she knew that she'd seen through his shell too.

"So I guess this dance is a long time overdue then," he said, holding out a hand.

She hesitated, but Frankie raised an eyebrow. "If we don't start dancing soon, I'm afraid that Mamma won't be able to enjoy her slice of cake."

"We wouldn't want that," Jill said. "It would go against my upbringing to deny someone from enjoying their dessert."

Frankie laughed. "It's settled then. A dance. For old times' sake."

"You make that sound as if this is a goodbye," Jill said, looking up at him.

His eyes looked sad for a moment before he smiled. "In a way it is. You've done your part. You came with me today. That was the deal."

She swallowed. That's what it was. Nothing more than that. Even when it felt like so much more.

chapter thirteen

"Frankie's here to see you," Carly announced as she walked into the kitchen the next morning. They'd only just opened for business, and Jill couldn't help but wonder what had brought on the urgent visit.

"You can send him back here," Jill told her sister. If she didn't keep working, she wouldn't get this batch of scones into the oven before the first batch sold out, as they were known to do on Sundays.

But that wasn't the only reason for wanting to talk to Frankie in the kitchen. Her sisters would be busy out front serving hungry customers. And she suspected that whatever Frankie had come to say was a private matter.

Carly disappeared again behind the door, and Jill smoothed her hands on her apron before resuming her task. A moment later, Frankie walked through the swinging door. He'd been back here before recently, when he'd personally picked up Nana's three-tiered wedding cake to carefully transport to Concetti's for the reception.

Now, though, he stuffed his hands into his pockets and looked around, seeming as out of place in her company as she suddenly felt in his. They both knew when he'd dropped her off last night that the spell had been broken. He'd offered to walk her to the door, being the gentleman that he was, and however tempting, Jill had declined, saying she'd be okay on her own.

Because she always had been, hadn't she?

"So this is where the magic happens," Frankie said, giving her a little smile.

"At least the baking," Jill said, pushing back the nerves that danced in her stomach. "Besides, didn't you come back here when you picked up my grandmother's wedding cake?"

"I guess I was too focused on the job to notice anything else that day." Frankie gave her a long look, one that seemed to cut straight through to Jill's inner voice.

The one that told her that she was guilty of the very same thing. Too often.

"Let me just get these scones in the oven and then I'll be all yours." She molded the dough onto the tray in a round, shape, scoring it into triangles.

"I won't take up too much of your time," Frankie said, once she had the tray in the oven and the timer set. "I owe you something."

Frankie held out a single piece of paper, folded in half, and Jill didn't need to open it to know what it was. She hesitated and then, knowing that Maria expected the recipe to be in the book, took it with a small smile.

"I know this wasn't easy for you," she said, but the truth was that it wasn't easy for her either. The wedding was over. And this recipe now felt like a final payment, a transaction between two business people, one that confirmed the end of the exchange.

"You earned it," Frankie assured her.

"Have you broken the news to your mother yet?" Jill asked, even though she wasn't sure she wanted to hear any of the details.

"No," he surprised her by saying. But just when her heart started to pick up speed, he added, "But I will tonight. Maybe after she's had a glass of wine." More seriously, he said, "I hate to think of disappointing her."

Their eyes met and Jill's heart began to race. She felt for a moment like he might be waiting for her to say something, and a part of her wanted to. That maybe, he didn't need to tell Maria anything. That maybe, they could just continue as they were.

But that wasn't the deal. And the recipe that she held in her hand was an irrefutable reminder that her role in Frankie's life was over.

"How many days do you think it will be until she reminds you about the girls from the wedding?" Jill asked, almost dreading the answer even though she was sure she knew it.

Sure enough, Frankie snorted. "Days? More like minutes."

"It was just a temporary solution then," Jill said. And a temporary arrangement, she reminded herself. But somehow, these last few weeks had felt like a new start, not something with a fixed ending.

Frankie looked thoughtful for a moment. "I'm not the only one free now. I'm sure there are plenty of men who would welcome your company."

"Oh." Jill huffed out a breath. If there were, she hadn't found them before. But then, she supposed, she hadn't exactly been looking, either. She'd been hiding. In the school bathroom. In this bakery kitchen. "Maybe. But right now the only guaranteed man in my life weighs about five pounds and he's covered in fur."

"Actually, Zach was asking about you," Frankie said slowly. He was giving her a strange look, maybe picking up on her shock.

"Zach? From the fire station?" Obviously, he was talking about Zach from the station if only because the only other Zach in town was about ten years old and liked to order their new cake pops.

But Zach Mason had never paid her any attention before. Never given her a second glance, really. Never offered to buy her a drink or chatted with her much on the nights that their group all got together. And he'd been almost rude last weekend when they'd gone to Jonah's new restaurant.

"Very funny," Jill said to Frankie, knowing a joke when she heard one. "More like he thought you were too good for me."

"Quite the opposite," Frankie replied, his tone showing that he was serious. "I think that he thought you were too good for me."

Jill tried to process what Frankie was saying and couldn't, mostly because there was no reason from what she could tell that Frankie would be undeserving of her affection.

Uninterested was another story. He had a type. One that looked like that girl Bianca at the wedding. Jill was sure within a week she'd be seeing Bianca at the tavern if she went for a drink with her sisters.

Maybe, it was best to stay home. Home where she couldn't feel hurt. Or wish for things that would never be.

"It's true," Frankie said. "He pretty much told me that he had a thing for you."

Jill could now tell that Frankie wasn't joking at all. That he was serious. But…Zach? He was tall. Handsome. Friends with Nick, which spoke to his character. A good, solid guy.

"He's never said so before!" Jill blinked quickly, trying to process this, thinking back on all of her encounters with him, which were friendly at best.

"Maybe he was working up the courage." Frankie shrugged. "Or waiting for the right time."

"I never thought about him in that way before," Jill replied. But then, she'd never thought of Frankie in a romantic sense either.

Now, she wondered if she'd ever get back to only seeing him in a casual light again.

Frankie stepped away from the worktop. "I don't want to take up too much of your time," he said.

"Oh." Jill swallowed hard, searching for a reason to keep him there for a few minutes. "Thank you, Frankie, for the recipe," she said sincerely. "It will mean so much to my grandmother. You'll see when you come to her party next weekend."

"I don't think it makes sense for me to go," Frankie said.

Jill tried to hide the disappointment from registering on her face, but she must not have succeeded because Frankie grimaced.

"If we're broken up, then wouldn't it be awkward?"

Jill hadn't thought about that until now, and with great reluctance, she nodded her head. This party was to celebrate Nana, and she didn't want anything to overshadow the event.

"My mother will be there though," Frankie said. "I'm sure that she'll apologize on my behalf. You might even get another flower delivery. Condolences this time."

Jill managed to laugh. But this time, it felt bittersweet.

"Nana will be happy to have her there." She was going for cheerful but something in her heart felt far from happy. "I won't play up my heartache over our breakup too much." She forced a smile.

"Well, now." Frankie straightened up. "It wouldn't be so bad to be a little sad that our relationship ended, would it? I mean, for believability's sake."

"Not so bad at all," she said.

Or, she realized as she looked him in the eye, too difficult.

Frankie opened his mouth and then, after a pause, closed it again.

"Well, I guess this is it," he said.

Jill nodded, sensing the awkwardness that hadn't been there just last night when they were dancing together under the watchful gaze of two dozen of Frankie's closest family members.

"I can still help out with Toffee," Frankie said suddenly.

Jill brushed a hand through the air. "I can't ask you to do that."

"I'm offering," Frankie said. "Besides, the truth is that I've become sort of fond of the little guy."

Jill nodded. "The feeling is mutual."

Their gazes met until she looked away and started clearing the mixing bowl from the counter. A moment later, she heard the door swing open and then closed again, and as much as she knew that when she turned back around, Frankie would be gone and she would be in this quiet kitchen alone again, the way she was used to, there was no comfort to be found in her old routine anymore.

Even though their relationship had been fake, something about their breakup felt all too real.

*

Frankie was true to his word, but then, that hardly came as a surprise to Jill. He took Toffee for a walk both Monday and Tuesday, each day leaving a bag of food from Concetti's waiting for Jill in her fridge when she returned in the evening.

But Wednesday, on her day off, he didn't stop by.

And after glancing at the clock and wishing for something that was never going to happen, Jill headed out with Toffee to her grandmother's house, where she'd promised to meet her sisters for lunch.

Robert, Nana's new husband, greeted her on his way out of the house.

"Jill! And little Toffee!" Always partial to dogs, Robert wasted no time in stooping down to admire him. "I didn't get to meet him the last time you visited." Then, with a twinkle in his eyes that even his spectacles couldn't hide, he added, "I hear you've been busy."

"I certainly have," Jill remarked. "But not in my usual way. This little guy has kept my attention from the bakery lately."

"Dogs will do that," Robert agreed. "They bring out the best in people."

"Are you joining us today?" Jill asked. She'd always liked Robert Quincy, even when he was just Nana's next-door neighbor, always hopeful for a date.

But Robert shook his head as he stood. "I'm headed over to Mapleton to meet up with my grandson," he explained. "We have a lot of decorations to put up before the party on Saturday."

"I imagine Becca will be heading over straight from lunch."

"You can count on it." Robert grinned but he stopped again before getting in his car. "It's good to see you so happy, Jill. Dogs are special, aren't they? They have a way of filling parts of our hearts that we didn't even know needed healing."

Jill looked down at Toffee, who stared up at her with his dark, round eyes, and she reminded herself that she was going to be okay. That sure, it had been nice spending time with Frankie, having someone to talk to after a long day, someone to banter with. Maybe even flirt with.

And the thought of going back to her old routine no longer felt comforting, but it also was no longer an option.

"Come on, little guy," she said to Toffee. "Let's go through the gate."

Her sisters and grandmother were already seated at the table in the garden when Jill locked the fence gate behind her. Toffee pulled against the leash until she released it from his collar, watching as he sprinted toward Sugar, who gave him a quick sniff before chasing him three full laps around the yard.

Jill was laughing by the time she sat down across from Nana in the sunny backyard where a tray of sandwiches was waiting in the center of the table.

"I just saw Robert," she said.

"Oh, he finally got to meet Toffee!" Nana sighed happily. "Though I have to say that your little pup looks like he's already grown since the last time you were here."

"I agree. He's at least an inch taller," Carly said, admiring him from across the yard.

"It must be all the treats that Frankie's been feeding him on the walks," Nana continued.

Jill picked up the pitcher of lemonade and poured herself a glass, pushing back the image of Frankie and his dimpled grin. The eyelashes that somehow she'd never noticed.

She did her best to keep her tone neutral, even when her heart was straining in a way it hadn't since those scary few months when she thought they might lose the bakery. "Yeah. Maybe."

Becca gave her a funny look and then said, "I can't stay long. Nana knows that I have to help Jonah get everything ready for Saturday."

"Did you already pick out what you're going to wear, Nana?" Jill asked, eager to keep the subject off of herself.

"Oh, I'm still deciding. Carly told me all about your shopping trip, though." Nana looked impressed, if not a little surprised. "I gather that you wore that dress to the wedding?"

"Wedding? What wedding?" Carly asked.

Jill sighed. She should have expected that Maria would have said something to Nana. But had she also told her the rest of the story?

Nana's eyes were clear and sharp on hers, and Jill suspected that Maria had told her every last detail, from the good to the bad.

"I went to Frankie's cousin's wedding," she explained to her sisters. "And I wore the new dress I bought with you, Carly."

"And you didn't tell us?" Carly remarked, looking a little stung.

"There was nothing to tell," Jill said vaguely, but then, seeing the hurt in her sister's eyes, she realized that she was wrong. There was something to tell. And share. And that she wasn't going to push her family away anymore.

"Actually, there's something I do want to tell you about, Carly," she started. She felt the guilt rise when Carly looked at her warily. "Something I've been wanting to tell you."

Now, Carly's expression transformed into one of hope.

"It's about Frankie…" Before her sister could get too excited, she said, "We're just friends. That's all we ever were."

Carly blinked a few times. "But—"

"Frankie and I were never a couple," she told them. She expected to feel relieved for finally clarifying everything to her sisters, but instead, she felt another wave of disappointment.

"What?" Carly gasped. "But—but—"

"We were pretending," Jill told her. She sighed and pushed away her lemonade, meeting Becca's squint of disbelief across the table. "Frankie needed a date for the wedding. He didn't want to be matched up with any of the girls that Maria had asked to be invited for him."

Although after seeing a few of them, Bianca in particular, he probably would have had a fine enough time. Mamma Maria would have still been happy.

And Jill would have still gotten the recipe for the cookbook from Maria herself.

It all would have worked out, even if she hadn't agreed to the ruse. But she had. And now, a part of her wished she hadn't nearly as much as she was strangely glad that she did.

"Yes, but you guys have spent other time together," Becca pointed out.

"Only because when Maria heard that we were spotted at the Rustic Tavern, she assumed there was more to it." Jill looked around the table, lifting an eyebrow.

"I guess we're all guilty of that," Carly said, giving her a smile of apology. "But you could have told us otherwise."

"Maybe I should have." Jill nodded, knowing that her sisters would have played along, or at the very least not told Maria. "But I saw how happy you all were for me."

"We were happy for you," Becca insisted. "But not because you had a boyfriend."

Jill frowned at Carly, but she just gave a little smile and

nodded. "It's true, Jill. We were just happy because you seemed so happy!"

A flashback to that kiss at Jonah's restaurant came rushing back, along with the feel of Frankie's big hand on her waist, pulling her in close on the dancing floor.

"Yes, well, it was fun, but Frankie and I were only ever friends," Jill insisted, banishing any further thought of that kiss.

"That's all it was?" Carly looked so crestfallen that Jill almost felt the need to comfort her.

If she didn't feel the need to comfort herself first.

"I have to say that you two were pretty convincing," Becca remarked. "I never pictured the two of you together before, but somehow, it fit."

Jill didn't say anything, because it was true. And because it didn't matter now, did it?

"Frankie's a nice guy," Jill told the table, but it was Nana's eyes that quietly met hers. Jill wondered if Nana was surprised. Or disappointed. But Nana's expression didn't give anything away, and she knew that the only thing she had from her grandmother right now was support.

"So what was it like? Having a boyfriend for a few weeks?" Carly quickly clarified, "Even in the pretend sense?"

"It was...nice," Jill admitted.

"Nice having a boyfriend or nice having Frankie as your boyfriend?" Becca asked.

Jill thought of what Frankie had said about Zach. About a possibility that she hadn't even considered...and still didn't.

Becca had asked the question that went straight to her heart. It wasn't having a boyfriend that had been so wonderful. It had been who the boyfriend was.

Even if it was just pretend.

"Well, I'm sure that Maria wasn't too happy to find out that Frankie was lying to her," Carly remarked.

"I don't think he ever told her that," Jill said, glancing at Nana. "I think he just told her that it didn't last. And that's the truth, after all."

Now Nana's expression did move, but not in judgment or dismay. If anything, Jill thought that her grandmother looked curious. And that no matter what she was thinking about the matter, she knew that sometimes, there was just nothing to be said. And everything to accept.

chapter fourteen

If Frankie thought that his mother had reacted badly to the news of Gia's wedding, it was nothing compared to her response to his so-called breakup with Jill Parker. Since Sunday, she'd worn black every day, and she kept her late husband's handkerchief clutched in her hand at all times unless she was cooking or serving customers.

The only person who had been happy to hear the news was Zach, who had pulled Frankie aside and asked if it would be okay if he asked Jill out to dinner sometime. And what could Frankie say? No?

He couldn't do that, even when a part of him wanted to do just that.

Now, as Frankie stood in the kitchen of the restaurant, preparing trays of lasagna that would sell out quickly as they usually did Saturday nights, he wondered if Zach had acted on his suggestion yet. If he'd asked Jill out. And if she'd said yes.

"Careful!" his mother called out as she pushed into the kitchen through the dining room. "You almost forgot the layer of cheese!"

Frankie looked down at the lasagna he was assembling and realized she was right—he'd started with another layer of pasta, skipping one of the most important parts of the recipe.

"Sorry," he said. "I must be distracted."

Mamma gave him a suspicious glance but said nothing more as she bustled about the kitchen. For the first time since last Sunday, she was not wearing black, but instead her favorite red dress, one she kept for special events and parties.

"Are you heading out soon?" Frankie asked. He knew that Nana Parker's birthday party was starting in an hour.

"You still staying home?" Maria countered.

"Someone has to take care of the customers tonight," he pointed out.

"It's only three," his mother pointed out. "And your cousin will be here. Besides, it shouldn't be a late night. If I didn't know better, I'd say that you're using this restaurant as an excuse again."

"Again?" He stopped building the lasagna and stared at her. "What do you mean by that?"

Mamma stepped over toward the counter and sighed. "Frankie, you've been distracted all week, not just today. I haven't seen those dimples since the wedding."

"I'm tired, Ma," he said, but when he met her eyes, he knew that there was no point in denying it. His mother knew him too well. She saw straight through to the truth.

"I think that you miss Jill," she remarked.

He hesitated and then shrugged his shoulders. "It doesn't matter what I feel, Ma. I told you—"

"Oh, I know what you told me," she said, waving away his words with her hands. "But I also know that you invited Jill to the wedding so that you didn't have to be matched up with any of the girls I intended for you to meet."

He stared at her for a moment, seeing the challenge in her dark eyes. "Why do you say that?"

"Because you and Jill Parker have been nothing but friends since you were babies," Mamma said. "You expect me to believe that suddenly you thought to ask her out on a date conveniently right before this wedding?"

Frankie couldn't help but grin. "I can't get anything past you, can I?"

"No," Mamma said firmly. "And that's why I know that something has been troubling you all week."

"Well, Ma, I was worried about you—" All that crying—but what had it been for if she knew that he hadn't been dating Jill?

Mamma sighed heavily. "You worry about me too much, Frankie. Don't you see?"

Frankie stared at her, trying to understand what she was saying, and then finally shook his head.

His mother gave a sad smile. "Ever since you were little, since your father died, it's been you and me. You stepped in and helped out in this kitchen, learning to cook so that I didn't have to do it all on my own. But you did more than that, too, Frankie. You made me keep smiling. You kept me laughing. You kept me going."

He reached out and squeezed her shoulder. He wasn't used to flattery, not from Mamma, even if she did like to tell him he was the best-looking guy in the state every now and again. But he knew she was his mother, that she was just saying that because she had to—but now he realized that it was because she believed it.

And she believed everything she was saying now, too.

"You took care of me, Frankie."

"We took care of each other," he insisted. He could still remember those weeks and months after his father died like it was yesterday. His mother's sisters visited, and neighbors, too. They were always surrounded by people who cared about them. Friends. Family. Community.

But at the end of the day, when everyone left, back to their own homes, it was just the two of them. The apartment felt more quiet, even though Mamma's personality had always filled it in the past. And Frankie longed for that laughter, the one that always made him smile. That assured him that she was happy.

And that so was he.

"But you also take care of everyone else," she said. "You're always there to lend a hand for a neighbor or a friend. You even volunteer at the fire department on your time off. You even walk that cute little dog of Jill's on what little time you could be spending on yourself. Don't think I haven't noticed." She raised an eyebrow.

No, Mamma didn't miss anything. Which was why Frankie wasn't sure why he'd thought he could ever try to get something past her. No matter how good-intentioned.

"But I enjoy all those things, Ma," he pressed.

Especially walking that little dog. He was a cute little thing, growing bigger by the day even though he was still small enough to fit in one of Frankie's hands.

"I know, and that's why I encourage you to do them. But I also encourage you to get out. To date."

He groaned. "And we're back to this?"

"Frankie." His mother paused for a moment—a first for her. And Frankie knew he'd better take what she said next seriously. "Do you know why I push so hard for you to find a nice girl?"

"Because you want me to have babies that you can bounce on your knee?" Frankie raised an eyebrow. Then, when she reached for a dishrag and swatted him with it, he said, "I know that you just want me to be happy, Ma. And it's all I want for you, too."

"But I am happy, Frankie!" Mamma widened her eyes and opened her arms. "I have this kitchen. This restaurant. Wonderful friends. Family. The most handsome son."

Frankie rolled his eyes.

"And I had true love." Mamma patted her heart. "I couldn't have asked for more. And that's all I want for you."

"I date all the time!" Frankie reminded her.

"And they never last," Mamma said. "Because you don't want them to."

"What?" Frankie was about to remind his mother yet again that she didn't exactly welcome any of those women with open arms, but her look was no-nonsense.

"You pick these girls that you know you don't have a connection with. Oh, sure, they may be pretty, or nice, but they're not your match, Frankie. They're not what you want by your side for the rest of your life."

Frankie considered her words and eventually shrugged. He'd dated one pretty girl after the next, each one nearly identical to the last. It had been easy to blame her for why he needed to end things—even when deep down he knew at the beginning that it wasn't going to last. That maybe, he didn't want it to.

"No, probably not," he conceded.

"And that's okay, Frankie. That's why I encourage you to keep putting yourself out there. Do you know why I've been crying all week, Frankie?"

Frankie grimaced against the image of Mamma's handkerchief pressed to her face, her eyes red and runny.

"Because I felt like I had failed you," she said.

"Mamma!"

But his mother put a hand up. "Frankie, you have worried so much about taking care of me that you have stopped thinking about yourself. What you want. What you need. You even invited Jill to that wedding just because you thought it would make me happy."

"But it did, Mamma—"

She gave him a little smile. "It did. But not for the reason you think, Frankie. I was happy because you were happy. Those two weeks you were spending time with Jill was the happiest I've ever seen you since…"

She didn't finish her sentence but he knew what she was going to say.

It was the happiest he'd been since his father had died. It was true, perhaps, and at first, he'd chalked it up to relief that his mother was finally off his back. But now he knew that there was more to it. That his connection with Jill might have been an act on the surface, but deep down, it was real. He hadn't opened the door to it, hadn't sought it out, or even hoped to find it. But somehow, it had found a way in just the same.

"I love you, Ma," he said, giving her a long hug.

"I love you, my boy," she said, holding him tight. Pulling back, she wiped at her eyes and smoothed her skirt. "Well, I'd better head out. I want to be there when they give Sharon her gift. You've heard what it is?"

Frankie nodded. He knew that his mother wouldn't have a problem with him contributing the recipe, not when she was such a close friend to Sharon Parker, and especially not when the cookbook would benefit a good cause.

"Our recipe will be at the very front, I imagine," Mamma said before Frankie could tell her what he'd done. "How could it not be when I contributed our pizza sauce recipe?"

Frankie's jaw slackened before he could form any words. "*You* gave the recipe to Jill?"

"I don't see why not," Mamma said. "I know it's special, but that's why it was right to include it. That recipe is what brings in our customers, what keeps the lights on, but more than that, it's what kept us going. Not just Concetti's the restaurant, but Concetti, the family. The legacy."

Frankie swallowed hard. "I promised to always uphold that legacy."

"And you have. Look at this restaurant, Frankie. It isn't just what we give to the community, it's also what they've done for us. Where would we be without the people of this town? We take care of them when they sit down to eat, but they take care of us so much more."

Frankie nodded, knowing it was true. That his father would have wanted it this way. That maybe, this was what he had been trying to tell him, all those years ago, when he told him to carry on the recipe.

Frankie had held on to the past so tightly that he hadn't been willing to open his heart to share the future with anyone—in any way.

"When?" he asked, needing to know. "When did you give Jill the recipe?"

"Oh, last week?" Maria didn't seem to make a big deal of it as she began rummaging through her handbag for her lipstick. "I can't remember the exact day. Before the wedding."

Before the wedding. Meaning that Jill had already gotten what she needed from him. She could have ended their deal then and there, let him go to the wedding on his own, or still offered, as a friend.

But she hadn't done any of those things.

"What time are you leaving for Sharon Parker's party?" Frankie asked his mother.

Maria looked at him in alarm. "In twenty minutes. Why?"

"Because I think if I joined you, it would make you happy," he said, giving her a grin. "And it would make me happy, too."

*

Jill stood near the bar of Jonah's bistro, which had been transformed with clusters of brightly colored balloons, arrangements of seasonal flowers, and of course, a beautiful birthday cake that Nana had insisted on making herself.

"You know that it's not customary to bake your own birthday cake," Jill told Nana when she came over to take a signature pink drink from the tray on the bar top.

"Would you really deny me that pleasure?" Nana said with a wink.

Jill felt a familiar rush of guilt tighten her chest. Not so long ago, she might have done just that, or at least tried her best to convince her grandmother not to take on the task.

But life was too short to deny yourself what you really loved—or what you really wanted.

And she knew that all too well, or should have.

"Have you spoken to Maria yet?" Nana asked as Jill's gaze rested on the woman wearing a beautiful red dress.

Jill fought back the disappointment she'd experienced when Maria walked in alone. Even though it had been discussed and even though it was part of the plan, Jill still couldn't help but see it as confirmation that her time with Frankie had come to an end.

"You didn't tell Maria, did you?" Jill asked. "About the ruse?"

"I didn't have to," Nana replied. "She already knew. All along, in fact."

"What?" Jill stared at her grandmother as her mind replayed the events of the past few weeks. "But…she was so convincing. So…happy."

Nana smiled. "She was. Because Frankie was so happy. And I felt the same way, watching you."

"Oh." Jill shook her head, but her grandmother just tipped her head.

"You liked spending time with that young man, didn't you?"

"Of course I did," Jill said with a shrug. "We've always been friends."

"And now you're something more."

Jill saw the hope in her grandmother's eyes and she understood for the first time exactly why Frankie would have wanted to convince his mother that there was ever something more going on between them than there was.

"No, Nana," she said gently. "Frankie and I are just friends. I'm sorry if I ever gave you the impression that there was any more to it."

"And I'm sorry, too," Nana said. "But not for the reason you might think. I thought that maybe you finally let yourself believe in love."

"Of course I believe in love," Jill scoffed. But one glance at Nana, and she knew that her grandmother saw right through to her heart. To her deepest fears. Greatest feelings. She'd been there for Jill all her life, witnessing the ups and downs. And all the moments in between.

"You may have tried to fool yourself, but you won't fool me, Jill," Nana said. "You can't hide in the bakery forever."

"But you did," Jill pointed out.

"I did," Nana said. "Because it was a safe space. A happy space. It was where my heart was. Or so I thought." She smiled. "But I found my love, Jill. I have Robert. You girls. Sugar. And before that, I had your grandfather. And your mother. And then I had a hole in my heart that no amount of baking or even friends in this community could fill. I thought they could, and for a while, I even convinced myself that they did, but that was just the story I told myself. It was easier than admitting the truth."

"The truth?" Jill stared at the woman who didn't have a dishonest bone in her body.

"You know why I stayed working at that bakery so long, even when my arthritis was making it nearly impossible?" Nana's gaze searched hers. "Because I was afraid, Jill. Afraid of losing the last thing I had. The last thing I'd allowed myself to have. That bakery was everything to me."

"Nana, I didn't mean to push you out—" Jill had been too busy guarding her grandmother, making sure she didn't overdo it. Keeping her safe. Keeping her with her, she supposed.

But she'd never meant to keep her from doing what she loved best. Or living her life to the fullest.

Even if that's what she'd done to herself.

"You gave me the kick in the pants I needed." Nana squeezed her hand. "And that's why I've given you one in return."

"What?" Jill almost laughed.

Nana sighed deeply and then reached up to stroke Jill's cheek. "Everyone says we're so alike because it's true. You and me, Jill, we hold on to the things we love for fear of what will happen if we don't. But when you're so busy holding on to the past or worrying about tomorrow, it doesn't leave much room for today. It doesn't leave much room for anything…or anyone."

Jill nodded, knowing that her grandmother, like always, was speaking the truth. Even when it hurt.

"I guess I've been afraid to let anyone in. To lose what I have. To lose even more."

"You let Toffee in," Nana pointed out.

"Only because I couldn't imagine walking away from him," Jill said. "Even though I'd just met him. I...couldn't lose him." A lump rose in her throat. "And someday I will."

"There's only one thing in life that never dies," Nana said.

Jill stared at her grandmother, searching her lined face for the answer.

"Love goes on and on." She set a hand on her heart. "It just takes new forms. Memories. Recipes." She grinned. "Loss is inevitable, honey," Nana said gently, her blue eyes filled with understanding. "The only way to avoid it is to avoid love. And wouldn't that be the emptiest life of all?"

Jill didn't dare to speak for fear of a tear slipping free.

"Sometimes, you have to lose something to realize just how much it meant."

Like Frankie. Jill knew. She'd allowed herself to feel sad, for the loss of something she'd come to enjoy. But now, as her eyes shifted to another spot in the room, the table where not so long ago she and Frankie had sat side by side, and shared one perfect kiss, she also knew that she wouldn't have missed out on that experience, even knowing the outcome.

"And sometimes," Nana continued, "you have to almost lose something to know just how much you want to hold on to it."

"You mean when we almost lost the bakery?" Jill asked, searching Nana's face.

Her grandmother's expression lifted into a smile. "Something bigger than the bakery, Jill." She lifted her chin. "Look."

Confused, Jill glanced over her shoulder, her breath catching when she realized what Nana meant.

*

Jill didn't even see Nana slip away as Frankie approached, looking cleaned up and handsome in khaki pants and the same button-down shirt he'd worn for their first date at the Rustic Tavern.

Make that their first drink. Alone. As friends.

But as his dark eyes locked hers and his mouth lifted into a hint of a smile, she knew that she could deny it all she wanted but her heart knew the truth.

It was a date. Even if she hadn't known it at the time. Even if she'd tried to fight it.

And she didn't want to push away the possibility of love anymore.

"Frankie." She swallowed hard. "I...didn't think you'd be coming."

"No excuse not to now," he said, glancing over to where his mother stood with Nana. "My mother was on to us the entire time."

"So I just heard." Jill shook her head in wonder. "But...but she was so convincing."

"She was." Frankie's gaze lingered on hers, his expression more serious than the usual grin he wore. "But then....so were we."

She swallowed hard, managing to nod. "I guess it was safe for you to come then, seeing as we don't have to pretend anymore."

"No, those days are over," he said.

Jill set her jaw. Yes, those days were over, and he'd just reminded her of that.

"Then why come?" she asked, noticing the way her tone betrayed her hurt.

Frankie frowned slightly. "It's your grandmother's birthday. You know what she means to Mamma."

Jill nodded. She did know. The feeling was mutual. But right now, standing here, in front of Frankie, with their pretend relationship now permanently a thing of the past, she felt the painful knowledge that not everything in life was mutual, or reciprocated. Love wasn't always fair.

But sometimes, it was worth it just the same.

"Well, you do want to keep Mamma Maria happy," she replied, again hearing the edge that had crept into her tone.

"I'm not here to make my mother happy," Frankie said. "I'm here because there's nowhere else I wanted to be today. Because I knew you'd be here. And because you make *me* happy."

Jill stared at him, her heart starting to pound against her chest.

"I thought maybe you'd be here with Zach," Frankie said, and just for a moment, she saw a hint of apprehension flit through his gaze.

"Zach?" Jill was surprised by his comment, even after what he'd said last weekend. "He and I are just friends."

"Isn't that all that we are?" Frankie asked.

She stared into his dark eyes, seeing the question that hung there, the one that she couldn't answer because she was no longer so sure.

"All we were," she said, giving him a small smile.

He grinned, showing both his dimples. "I was hoping you would say that."

"And I was hoping you would," she said, smiling broader. Straight from the heart.

"We have a lot in common," he said, inching toward her. "I used to think you were too serious. Now I know...you're the kind of girl who takes things seriously. And I was hoping that maybe, you might consider taking us seriously."

Her breath caught as he inched toward her until they were face to face, hips against the bar, the crowd a blur around them.

"Frankie." She blinked quickly, feeling the emotions that she'd pushed away for so many years finally coming to the surface, aching to break free, to spread their wings, to open her heart. To love.

"Frankie, haven't you made me wait long enough?" Mamma Maria called out, and everyone in the room started to laugh.

Even Jill. Even though there was nothing funny about this. To stand here, on display, in front of all their closest friends and family. Letting someone in. Daring to fall.

"I think she wants us to kiss," Jill whispered.

Frankie cocked an eyebrow. "I am a pretty good kisser."

She could only shake her head, but there was no denying the truth. "You are. And I should know."

"Ah, so you liked that kiss, did you?" he said, closing the distance between them. "Maybe it's not so bad, then, kissing in front of an audience."

"You wouldn't want to disappoint your mother," Jill teased him, even as her heart began to pound in anticipation.

"Or myself," Frankie said. "I've been wanting to do this ever since the last time we were here."

Jill pulled in a breath. She didn't know what tomorrow would bring. Or next week. Or next month. And instead of being scared by that, she felt a little excited.

She just knew what could happen here. Now.

"Then what are you waiting for?" she whispered, looking up at him as everything and everyone else around her disappeared.

"You," Frankie said, giving her a slow grin right before his mouth met hers. "All this time, I was waiting for you."

About the Author

Olivia Miles is a *USA Today* bestselling author of feel-good women's fiction with a romantic twist. She has frequently been ranked as an Amazon Top 100 author, and her books have appeared on several bestseller lists, including Amazon charts, BookScan, and USA Today. Treasured by readers across the globe, Olivia's heartwarming stories have been translated into German, French, and Hungarian, with editions in Australia in the United Kingdom.

Olivia lives on the shore of Lake Michigan with her family.

Visit www.OliviaMilesBooks.com for more.